Last Light Ascending

Last Light Ascending

MICHAEL S. WHITING
JAYLIN WHITING

RESOURCE *Publications* · Eugene, Oregon

LAST LIGHT ASCENDING

Resource Publications
An Imprint of Wipf and Stock Publishers
199 W. 8th Ave., Suite 3
Eugene, OR 97401

www.wipfandstock.com

PAPERBACK ISBN: 978-1-7252-5487-9
HARDCOVER ISBN: 978-1-7252-5488-6
EBOOK ISBN: 978-1-7252-5489-3

01/04/21

To the Eternal Light Creator and all who past, present, and future strive to spread His light.

Micah 6:8

Acknowledgments

The idea behind this book was truly a family affair, so we first want to acknowledge the other half of our family team, Julia and Chase, for suggesting ideas for the plot and the development of characters (and a better ending—ha!).

Thank you to Krissi Dallas, a gifted fiction author and fantasy lover, for agreeing to read and review our manuscript prior to publication. You have been such a big supporter of our book the entire process, and we greatly appreciate it. Thank you for being such an inspiration to me (Jaylin). You have taught me so many things about the writing world. You're still one of my favorite teachers and thanks for putting up with my many Team Caleb comments, LOL. Love you!

Thank you to all of our Instagram followers—@light.creators—for being such big supporters of this entire journey from the very beginning. You've encouraged us in more ways than one through all of your comments, likes, and story replies. We love your enthusiasm, and we hope you enjoy the book for which you've been waiting so patiently.

Thank you to Wipf & Stock for accepting our book concept for publication and giving a father and daughter this memorable opportunity to co-author and publish a work of fiction together.

To our readers that pick up this book, we appreciate YOU for the support that you give just by reading it through to the end (and for giving it and us a chance!).

Finally, to our Lord who said "Let light shine out of darkness," the Author and Giver of life who knows all our next chapters.

Chapter 1

She held out her hands in front of her, wandering aimlessly in the darkness. As she ran through the hills, her dress snagged and tore on branches, her face and arms were cut and scraped, and she stumbled over rocks trying desperately to get away. Her heart raced as she could feel the quickening presence of her pursuers, and they were drawing closer.

"You cannot hide from us, light creator!" yelled out a raging, low, and terrifying voice.

Her foot suddenly tripped on a stone, and she tumbled to the ground. She pulled herself up quickly, and began crawling away on her hands and knees, feeling her hands along a large stone until she could sit up with her back against it, holding her breath, trying not to move, and listening. She heard low, mumbling voices coming closer before she could start making out what they were saying.

"He wants her alive," one of them said.

"She is the last one," said another.

She held in the compulsion to scream out, knowing full well that no one was near to help her. After a few moments, silence fell, except for the eerie sound of the wind moving through the trees and the pelting of a slow, cold rain that began to fall.

She heard them begin to move away, and after waiting a little while longer, she started to slowly inch her bruised body forward.

Suddenly, she felt a hand tightly grip around her ankle and drag her across the rough ground, laying her down like a captured animal in front of the other three ominous figures whom she could not see in the darkness but whose sinister presence she could sense. Though they moved about and spoke to one another as if alive, they carried with them the feeling of death. Whether from fear or utter exhaustion, she felt her consciousness begin to slip away.

"Where is she?" Erikai demanded sternly, entering the narrow, torch lit hallway.

"This way, my lord," came a low, growling hiss from the shadows. Into the light appeared a very tall, but thin, wispy figure covered with a long, black robe frayed on the ends that draped loosely on the floor. "We found her in the hills, trying to escape," it sneered.

Erikai followed the Shadow Man down the corridor through a doorway and into a dark room where the woman lay in a heap on the floor.

"Naomi, Naomi," Erikai said with a sound of mocking pity in his voice. "You knew I would find you." He crouched down in front of her and lifted her chin delicately with his hand. Her dark hair hung messily, covering much of her face, her greenish grey eyes piercing into his.

"Erikai, how could you do this?" she said as tears streamed down her dirty and disheveled face.

Erikai smiled softly, gently pushing her hair back away from her face and eyes, and then he stood up to his feet and walked over to a narrow window, peering off into the darkness of the valley below dotted with dim flickering firelight in the distance.

"I'm finishing what my father started, Naomi. I'm really sorry it had to come to this, but I warned you. You are the last one, and once you are no longer in the way, everything can be made right again," he said coldly. He turned back around as a crooked smile formed on his mouth. "And with me as king."

"King? We have never had a king," she answered with a weary sigh. "And you would plunge this world back into darkness?"

Naomi gasped, struggling to push herself up. "And what's to become of Tristan?"

"Tristan? The boy won't remember the world any other way," he responded defiantly, "and when he is ready, it will be his, and he will defend it for me."

"This world does not belong to anyone, Erikai. It belongs to all! And what kind of world will you leave to him?"

Erikai turned his back to her to face the window but did not respond.

"And you may get rid of *me*," Naomi said, weakly pushing herself up to her feet, "but the light is more than me, more than the others you have killed. You cannot extinguish it forever. It will find a way to ascend just like it did ages ago."

Erikai walked back to her, shaking his head. He placed his hand gently on her shoulder and whispered into her ear, "We shall see. Farewell, Naomi."

Erikai turned to leave the room, looking up toward the Shadow Man who had been hovering near the doorway. "Do it quickly," he said low under his breath.

"It shall be done, my lord," it said ferociously, bowing in approval.

Then, the door slammed shut behind him and Naomi's cries could be heard faintly as Erikai sauntered across a spacious central hall, his footsteps echoing loudly across the marble stone floor as he proudly passed by ruins of statues that had once lined the walls. He entered into a smaller room off to the side and approached the cries of a baby boy. Erikai lifted the child swaddled in a warm, furry blanket gently out of his crib, kissed him on the cheek and said proudly to him as he lifted him up, "My dear Tristan, prince of our new world."

Chapter 2

"Zeph . . . Zephyr, wake up, son," came a soft voice that roused him from his sleep. "I'm sorry to wake you, but I need you to go to the market. I used up the last of our luminai last night," said the boy's mother.

Zeph grunted as he sat up, rubbed his eyes, and climbed slowly out of bed to begin dressing himself in warm, thick layers, the embers of a dying fire still flickering nearby.

"What do we have to trade for it this time?" he asked, running a hand through his thick brown hair.

"Go see Elbor and ask how much you can trade for these," she said. He followed his mother out into the center of the small, candle-lit cottage where she had laid out various copper and silver objects on the table.

"Elbor," Zeph grumbled as he eyed the items and began loading them into a bundle and stuffed them into his shoulder pack. "That fat, old man never trades fairly."

"We don't have a choice, son. We can't get luminai without him."

"You said he knew my father once. Then why won't he help us?"

"He trades for Erikai. Besides, he has to make his own way in this world, Zeph. Don't you want anything to eat before you go?" she asked while Zeph put on his long coat and began to lace up his boots.

"You mean the same gruel we had for dinner?" Zeph retorted with a smirk. "I'll be fine," he said as he threw the pack over his shoulder, kissed his mother on the forehead, and grabbed a long, wooden staff leaning against the wall beside the door.

"Please be careful, Zeph," she said as he stepped out of the cottage and into the frosty air.

Zeph turned back toward her and waved before pulling out his small luminai torch and turned away to start down the long, dark lane of firelit cottages. His feet crunched over a thin layer of snow on the ground.

The sky was dark and the air was filled with a smoky, grey haze coming from the wood-burning fires in the village of Adelaide. A few people greeted Zeph as he passed by. Others glared at him as if in a daze, their faces dimly lit in the shadows as a sharp, sweet aroma emanated from the vapor of root weed pipes.

Zeph's thoughts went back to the last time he had met with Elbor, which had not ended well. With every step, Zeph could feel the dull pain in his side from a recent altercation he had with a gang of older boys. Several of them were sent away with their own injuries, but Zeph had come home empty-handed. He grasped his staff tighter, determined not to let it happen again.

The world was always cold. A subterranean stone called luminai, remnants that had fallen long ago from a nearby dying star, provided the world enough warmth for survival and allowed some forms of food to grow. But the people were desperately poor. Most animal life had died off or was used for food and clothing.

Luminai was the world's most precious resource. When heated, its properties burned much brighter, longer, and warmer than fire or candlelight. When King Erikai discovered its value, he took control of the supply and production, enslaving the strongest men from all the villages to work in mines and appointed a merchant trader in each village.

There were four villages spread out on one large island: Varkos, which was the largest, was due straight east in the center and a few hours journey from Erikai's palace; Adelaide lay farther to the south and east. Rosten was by far the poorest of the villages and was the farthest eastward and closest to the Bleak Mountains. Riskolde sat to the north along the rugged coastline.

Zeph's father, Daeron, was among the many men who were taken from Adelaide. He was enslaved within a year after Zeph was born and was never seen or heard from again. Like so many young men growing up in a dreary world without a father, Zeph had developed a thick skin and a hardened attitude early on, which defied his otherwise smaller stature.

Zeph came upon Adelaide's bustling marketplace already filled with local merchants buying, selling, and trading their goods. All over, fires warmed and illuminated the crowded square with tall lamp posts dispensing torchlight on the sea of people below. From the corner of his eye, Zeph spotted a few of Erikai's armored guards patrolling the perimeter of the market as he pressed his way through the noise and commotion of the square toward a narrow alley of shops.

Upon arriving at Elbor's, Zeph walked in and noticed a few people milling about in the tight-knit space of shelves stocked with various items for trade. Zeph pretended to be interested in something on one of the shelves, peering out of the corner of his eye and waiting for the others to leave before approaching Elbor who sat in a candlelit corner sorting through a deck of irregular-shaped playing cards.

"Ah, Zeph. How are you, my boy?" said the heavy-set Elbor gruffly through his curly red beard, looking up with greedy delight.

"Not bad, Elbor," replied Zeph reluctantly, gritting his teeth.

"I know what you're here for, son," he leaned forward and whispered, "but I ain't got any. You're too late this time, I'm afraid," Elbor grinned as he peered past Zeph's shoulder into the far corner of the shop. Zeph immediately felt a pair of eyes staring at his back and turned around to see someone stepping out from the shadows towards him.

"How much do you want for it?" Zeph sighed.

"Too much to trade with the likes of you," the soft, female voice came back, provoking and confident. Elbor chuckled in the background.

"Why don't you see what I've got to trade first?" Zeph said as he began to remove and open his shoulder pack.

"Sorry, I'm not giving it up," she answered defiantly.

Zeph pleaded aggressively, "I only need a little. My mother is not going to be happy if I come home empty-handed."

"You mean empty-handed *again*?" she corrected him coldly.

At that moment, their attention was drawn towards a few buyers who walked in through the doorway of the shop. Immediately, Zeph's antagonist grinned, turned quickly, and dashed out into the street. Elbor burst into rollicking laughter as Zeph, without a moment's hesitation, hastened in pursuit.

Zeph raced through the maze of merchant stalls, bumping past buyers and knocking over boxes and carts with his eyes fixed on the object of his chase. For a brief moment, he lost sight of the runner in the crowd and then spotted the gate at the far end of the square, which led out from the village and up into the hills, just as it was closing shut.

The light of Zeph's luminai torch was dying out as he left behind the market square and made his way up into the thick darkness of the hills, hiking through clusters of lifeless, tangled trees. Zeph gripped his long staff readily as he listened for sounds of movement.

"You can't have it," called out the voice from the darkness.

"Well, I have a torch, and you have luminai," replied Zeph as he tried to follow the voice to its source. "Neither of us can see where we are going too well. So why can't we just work it out where we both go home happy?"

"Where's the fun in that?" she yelled, as Zeph felt something brush past him. He quickly turned to see a shadow hastening back down toward the gate to the square. Reacting instantly, he dropped his staff and reached out his hand to grab hold of the runner.

"I got you, *Laney*!" Zeph said victoriously. A young girl spun around, her light brown hair flowing out from underneath a long, dark blue cloak. She gave Zeph a playful jab into his gut that made him wince.

"I almost made it, Zeph!" she said with a spirited laugh. Zeph released her and stooped to pick up his staff.

"Afraid of getting jumped again, are we?" she teased.

"Yeah, thanks a lot," said Zeph as he rubbed his sore ribs.

"Sorry about that," she mused.

"No big deal. Where's Wiggin?" Wiggin was Laney's noctambule, a chubby creature with thick brown fur, large earwings, and round yellow eyes. Zeph found the creature endearing.

"He's at home. Let's take a walk up to the overlook."

Laney pulled from her belt a small thin blue rod of luminai and gave it to Zeph who placed it in his torch and lit it. He looked into Laney's face as it was lit up by the luminai and smiled. Together they walked farther up the hill and away from the distant village of Adelaide below.

Reaching the top, they walked through the crumbled walls and broken archways that remained of an old abandoned stone house overgrown with dark vines. They sat together on a ledge, peering down the hill toward the faint glow of Adelaide's busy market below and the rows of surrounding cottages.

As Laney talked, Zeph listened intently. When she smiled, he smiled. They had grown up together. She was his only real friend, and she always seemed to know what he was thinking. He always felt a special warmth around her. They had become so close over time that he felt completely comfortable in her presence.

"Tell me about that dream you had again," Laney requested, interrupting his contemplation. "You know, about how the world was beautiful and bright and full of music. Do you think it was really like that once? I just can't imagine it," said Laney staring in the direction of Adelaide. Zeph looked at her with eyes of admiration and curiosity.

"I shared that dream with my mother," Zeph said, looking down, "but she told me never to talk about it anymore. I think it reminds her of my father."

"My parents won't speak of the past either. No one ever talks about the way things were. They're all afraid the Shadow Men are hidden among us, listening to our every word, because King Erikai fears rebellion."

"While he lives in that big, fancy palace lit up day and night controlling the supply of luminai, we all just turn on each other. It doesn't make sense."

"You've seen Shadow Men take people away from our village who never return. They could be hiding anywhere, and . . . "

"Yeah, I know. They can't be stopped." Zeph pulled up a stalk of root weed nearby and started twiddling it between his fingers.

"You're not smoking that now, are you?" she asked.

"Now you sound like my mother, Laney. And no, I'm not."

"That stuff does strange things to a person. It makes them see things."

"Well, it might make things feel just a little bit better in this awful place for a while," said Zeph bitterly, flicking the weed away and brushing his hands off.

Laney started to hum. Zeph loved it whenever she sang. His bitterness left him, and now all that mattered was that he was beside her. He no longer cared about the cold or the darkness, about the Shadow Men, about Erikai. Being next to her was enough.

"We should get home," Zeph said. "But how about that luminai?"

"A few rods for your torch. That should last you and then you can have it back. Maybe," said Laney grinning.

They made their way back down the hill into the center of Adelaide. Zeph walked with her to the start of the pathway toward her home, but before they parted, Laney held out her hand. Zeph reached out to grab it, but stopped after she blushed and said, "Your torch?" Zeph reluctantly handed it to her as she slyly handed him a few luminai rods.

"Thanks," he said as he turned to walk away, "and my mother thanks you, too."

"You know, I almost got away from you this time," she said, squinting her eyes wryly at him.

"Well, I guess I'll see you tomorrow, Laney?"

"If you can catch me first," she replied with a smile that lit up her face, anticipating the challenge. As she said goodbye and walked inside her cottage, shutting the door behind her, Zeph was reminded of a memory of Laney from his childhood and a tender smile formed on his lips.

A young Zeph, not yet ten years of age, walked home from the market with his torch in hand, kicking his feet through the thin layer of snow as he went. As he turned down the lane, dimly illuminated by the light from the surrounding cottages, he heard the faint sound of a child singing but couldn't trace from where it was coming. Zeph stopped for a moment and then let out a heavy sigh before resuming his pace.

"What's wrong with you?" a voice inquired.

He looked over to the side of the road and was surprised to see a little girl his age sitting in the shadows by herself, drawing in the snow with a branch. Her hair fell a little past her shoulders, and her soft brown eyes seemed to be searching Zeph's face intently.

"I'm fine," Zeph shrugged, slightly embarrassed. "What are you drawing?"

"Well, come here and see," she invited him warmly.

Zeph walked over to her side, stooping down and holding his torch just above them. "What is that?" he asked.

"Well, it's uhm, uh . . . what do you think it looks like? Hey, you want to see something?" She pulled out two thick pieces of luminai from inside her cloak.

"Where did you get those?"

"Shhhh," she motioned for Zeph to move in closer as she whispered, "I stole them."

"You stole—?" Zeph began to say, but Laney put her hand over his mouth.

"I'm just kidding, silly," she giggled. "Do you want one?"

"Well, yeah," Zeph exclaimed quietly, "but you need to be careful. If someone saw you alone on the street with these . . . "

"Oh, they couldn't catch me," the girl interrupted, as she held out one of the pieces for Zeph to take before quickly snatching it back.

"You'll have to catch me first!" she said as she gave him a light jab and took off running down the lane away from him, her cloak flowing behind her. Zeph followed but soon lost sight of her.

"Where'd you go?" Zeph called out, stopping to catch his breath. The streets were empty and silent except for a few people walking by pushing their carts through the snow and eyeing Zeph curiously.

Suddenly he felt a hand grasp the back of his coat, and he jumped.

"Ha ha! Did I scare you?" she asked, laughing.

"No," Zeph insisted, his face blushing.

"Sure seemed like it to me," the girl answered, her eyes narrowing, calling his bluff, and she sped off in the opposite direction.

Zeph caught up to her just as she turned to run up the stairs of one of the cottages.

"I got you!" he said, grabbing on to her arm as she spun around to meet his eyes.

"I made it home, so I'm safe," she said, celebrating with a dance at the top of the stairs. The door opened behind her, and a woman's face with a stern expression leaned out, "Laney!" she exclaimed, looking suspiciously at Zeph. "Where have you been? Get inside. You shouldn't be out by yourself either, young man. Now get home."

"Laney's your name?" Zeph asked as she turned to leave.

"Yep!" she responded. "And yours is . . . ?"

"Zephyr."

She let out a sweet laugh. "Can I just call you Zeph?"

He nodded in agreement, smiled, and said, "Maybe I'll see you tomorrow, Laney?"

"Maybe. If you can catch me first," she said, her mouth curling into a delicate smile as she followed her mother into the cottage.

Chapter 3

The door to the throne room burst open and in walked a well-built young man dressed head to toe in a dark hooded cloak. He strutted across the central hall to where King Erikai sat drinking from an ornate goblet.

"Father, there is word of unrest in Varkos," said Tristan, approaching Erikai and kneeling at the foot of the steps. "Shall I investigate?"

Erikai turned to one of the Shadow Men and motioned with his hand. "Find the meaning of this and do something about it," he said sternly.

"Yes, my lord," one of the Shadow Men replied, turning to leave the room with several armored guards. Tristan, his head still hanging low, peered up from under his hood to see a Shadow Man glare at him as it passed by.

"I don't understand, father," said Tristan once he and Erikai were alone. "I would have gone for you."

Erikai descended the steps toward Tristan and removed his son's hood revealing a head of wavy blonde hair. He peered proudly into his son's scruffy but handsome face and greenish grey eyes. Then, grabbing Tristan firmly by the shoulders, Erikai lifted him up to his feet, saying, "I know, son, and I thank you, but I wanted to see you."

Tristan was surprised by his father's tone. He followed him up the stairs, but Erikai stopped half way and motioned for Tristan to sit beside him.

"Son, I have been thinking a lot about the future, and I know I have a worthy successor sitting right here with me," Erikai said with a warm smile. "I'm proud of you. You are a great warrior and have shown great promise as the future king of this world. I am glad to know that our world will be safe and secure in your hands when my time comes."

"You know I have only ever wanted to do what pleases you," said Tristan. "I will make you proud, and I will defend what is ours with my life. I promise."

"Yes, I know," Erikai said agreeably. "I also know you've heard the whispers and rumors. They are just stories, but we have to stay vigilant, my son. Hope is a powerful weapon, and if the people are led to believe . . . You must subdue any trace of rebellion among the people of the villages with the help of the Shadow Men."

"The Shadow Men cannot be trusted," interrupted Tristan boldly.

"Funny, that's what they have said about you," replied Erikai, his face hardening and then softening again. Erikai leaned in closer to Tristan and said, "I think they are jealous of my favor towards you, son."

"And after you are gone?" Tristan asked.

"You'll need them, and they'll need you. I have done all I can to protect what is ours. All that I ask is that you defend it in honor of my memory. All I have done has been for you." Erikai reached over and embraced Tristan. "For you, my son. Do you understand?"

"And I am grateful, father. Haven't I proved that?"

"Yes, indeed you have. There is no one I trust more. Your mother, too, would be proud," Erikai said as he took in his hand the long, silver necklace that hung around Tristan's neck and pulled it in closer. His thoughts wandered off momentarily into the past. "Hm, but about these rumors," he suddenly continued, dropping the necklace, "you must do all that you can."

"I will," replied Tristan.

"Then go rest, my son. You have earned it."

The words of his father echoed in Tristan's mind as he left the hall, fingering the silver necklace and wishing he had known his mother.

Chapter 4

Zeph's mother was pleased to see that he had returned with more luminai and noticed the visible change in his disposition.

"You saw Laney again, didn't you?" she said, smiling.

Zeph blushed. "What makes you say that?"

"I can always tell. You are a different person around her. You always have been, even since you two were little children. She is a lovely girl," his mother said, winking at him.

"She's a friend, mother. My only friend," he said, rolling his eyes.

Zeph's mother just shook her head with a knowing smile, and she took the hot kettle from the fireplace and filled two bowls on the table full of a thick, steaming, greyish stew. Zeph lit several small lanterns around the house with the luminai, and in a few minutes the room brightened and warmed as Zeph began to empty his pack.

"How did . . . ?" his mother began to ask, surprised to still see the objects she had sent with him to trade.

"I didn't have to trade. Laney . . . she traded one of her rods for my torch. It should be enough for us for now, but we should use it sparingly. Elbor is out of his supply."

"She obviously cares for you," said his mother, eyeing him closely with tender curiosity while Zeph's eyes shifted down as he ate silently.

"So how is Elbor?" his mother asked after a while to break the awkward silence.

"Same as ever. How did he know my father? You've never told me more than that."

"It was a long time ago, Zeph," she answered, dodging his eyes and glancing away. "You know I don't like to talk about it." She shifted uneasily and then stood up from the table. With her back to him, she stirred the stew over the fire, as Zeph fought back the urge to press the question further. Every time he would mention his father, it made her visibly uncomfortable, and she always refused to talk about the past.

That night, Zeph lay down replaying the conversation with his mother as well as his day spent with Laney. He slept deeply and had a vivid dream, images and flashes of faces and people he did not know. A warm, beautiful light seemed to emanate from them, and they were sharing it with everyone around them.

Zeph was surrounded by a world alive with color—a deep blue sky above, light green grass on the hills, beautiful budding trees with long fruit-bearing branches, and all kinds of blossoming flowers displaying various shades of color. A soft melody sung by haunting voices filled the air. It seemed that the world was moving in sync to the pleasant music.

Suddenly the music stopped and an ominous dark cloud filled the sky and a deep shadow covered the whole land. The vegetation withered and the people disappeared. Zeph was left standing alone in darkness. Nothing moved. Then, he saw a bright hand reaching out towards him. He took it, and as soon as he touched it, he felt a strange surge of incredible warmth and energy pulsating through his entire body. It was almost painful, as if he couldn't contain it, but he felt more alive than ever. His eyes were blinded with brilliant light, and he woke up suddenly. The light faded away as he returned to the darkness of his cold room and to the sound of a low, crackling fire.

A soft tapping on his bedroom window caught his attention. At first he ignored it, but then it continued and became louder. Zeph crept across the cold floor to peer out the window, seeing a figure in the shadows holding a luminai torch and standing in front of the door to their cottage. It was Laney.

Zeph pushed open the frosted window. "What are you doing here, Laney? You shouldn't be out by yourself now."

"I can't find him," she whispered intently.

"Wiggin?" Zeph asked. "I'll be out in a moment." Zeph checked to make sure his mother was asleep before he returned to his room, dressed quickly, and hurried quietly outside.

"Where did you see him last?" he asked as they started off down the path together.

"I woke up cold, saw the window was open, and then noticed he was gone."

"Well, last time your father found him in those caves. I bet we'll find him there again."

"Oh, I dread having to go to that place again, Zeph." She took his hand as a soft delicate snow began to fall, and he felt a burst of exhilaration sweep over him.

"You know, I had that dream again, Laney," Zeph said after a few moments of walking in silence, "except this time it felt even more real than before."

"Do tell," said Laney, excitedly.

"It's hard to explain really. I saw faces again, people I didn't know. There was a beautiful valley, full of light, full of color. I felt weightless . . . at peace. And then darkness came, and it all went away. Except . . . "

"Except what?"

"Except this time it ended differently." The snow began to fall faster. "There was a hand. A bright hand surrounded by the warmest light I've ever felt. It was like the light was coming out of it. I touched it and then . . . "

"What?" Laney insisted.

"I felt . . . everything and nothing. I felt . . . complete."

"I don't understand," she replied.

"I don't either. I don't know what it all means."

The two turned south away from the village, ascending over a rocky hill and across an immense barren field that led toward a line of tall cliffs that rose up and then fell gradually to the coast some distance away. No one ever ventured out to this uninviting wasteland.

"I think I hear him," said Zeph as they got closer, the sounds of a shrill screech heard coming from inside one of the caves. Zeph held the torch out in front of them as the snow continued to fall slowly and steadily. They climbed cautiously up the side of the cliff and entered the damp cavern, walking deeper inside until Zeph spotted Wiggin hovering near a section of the wall covered with a mound of stones.

"Wiggin!" Laney called out, whistling to him, and he immediately flew to perch on her outstretched arm, crawling up onto her shoulder and licking her face. "What were you thinking flying off like that again?" she asked as she gently stroked his chin. His short, stubby tail wagged happily.

Zeph walked closer to the wall where they had found Wiggin, noticing a narrow shaft of colorful, warm light protruding out from between the stones.

"What is it, Zeph?" Laney asked.

Zeph didn't answer. He just handed Laney the torch and began to remove the stones. As he did the light became brighter and warmer until Zeph could see an opening inside the wall that led deeper into a hidden pathway.

"Do you see this, Laney? There's some kind of light in there."

Gripping Laney's hand tightly, she resisted and pulled back. "Wait . . . are you sure?"

"We have to go in there," Zeph insisted.

Laney didn't say a word but followed Zeph into the confined corridor along a winding path until it opened up into a much larger room with a deep pit dug out in the center of the floor. The mysterious light seemed to be emanating up from the pit, at the bottom of which Laney and Zeph saw a mound of skeletons.

"That strange glow seems to be coming from those bones. This must be some kind of tomb," she said. There was only a thin ledge that surrounded the pit. "There's nowhere to go," Laney's voice echoed.

All at once, Wiggin flew off Laney's shoulder up into the open space of the room. "Wiggin!" she cried. As Zeph reached out to grab for him he began to slip down into the pit. He swung his body around fast to try and grab a hold of the edge and dug his feet hard into the side but dropped the torch down into the pit.

"Zeph!" Laney cried out as she reached to pull Zeph back up, but as the torch hit the bottom of the pit, a surge of bright, warm light shot up, causing Zeph to lose his footing again and fall backwards hard on the pile of bones. The light in the pit became blinding before he passed out and everything faded to darkness.

The next thing Zeph heard was Laney's voice calling his name. Zeph struggled to pull himself up to a sitting position. His vision was blurred, and his head throbbed from the fall as he brushed himself off. The room had darkened except for the glow of the luminai torch that lay near him.

"I'm all right," he yelled up to her. Zeph carefully climbed his way back up to where Laney stood waiting with Wiggin who had returned and was resting on her shoulder.

She pulled him up onto the ledge, her eyes alight with wonder and confusion. "Did you feel that? It was so beautiful. I could see like never before. So many colors. And the cave shook. And it was warm and it felt like . . . like . . . "

"Like the light was inside you?" Zeph finished her thought. "That's how my dreams made me feel, like there is this harmony between everything." `

"I think I understand how your dreams made you feel."

"We need to get back," said Zeph, but at the same time, neither of them wanted to leave.

Who were these bodies? Who put them here? What caused the strange light? Zeph thought to himself. The same questions swirled in Laney's mind as they made their way back to the mouth of the cave, down the cliffside, and back across the barren field toward Adelaide.

Chapter 5

Tristan marched through the streets of Adelaide carrying a luminai staff. The people bowed before him as his long dark cloak dragged behind him followed by Shadow Men and several armored guards. Those remaining in their cottages cowered in fear but were all pushed forcefully into the streets to be questioned.

The people feared Tristan. His serenity was disarming, even terrifying, for someone they had come to associate with their suffering and slavery. There was a power in his presence, yet it was mysteriously constrained. Erikai rarely showed himself to the villagers. Although the people trembled around the Shadow Men, they were in awe of Prince Tristan and feared him the most.

Zeph's mother was in her cottage pacing back and forth when she heard a rapid knocking at the door.

"Navilda! It's us. Laney's gone," called a voice from the other side. Zeph's mother opened the door and quickly pulled Laney's parents inside. Prince Tristan was just several cottages away.

"So is Zeph," she replied with concern.

"Wiggin is also gone," said Laney's mother. "They must have gone looking for him, but they haven't come back yet. Prince Tristan is on his way, and they are questioning everyone in the village about the strange light. What are we going to do?"

"I don't know," Navilda responded.

All at once, a bony hand reached out from the shadows and dug into Zeph's mother's neck, growling in a low hiss, "Come. Now!"

The Shadow Man dragged Navilda outside and led her before Tristan. "This one, Prince, has something to tell you."

"Take her into the center of the market with the others. All of them," Tristan demanded.

Zeph and Laney returned to the outskirts of Adelaide, but before they could get closer to see what all the commotion was about, Elbor spotted them and pulled them out of sight.

"Where have you two been?" he demanded.

"What is going on, Elbor?" asked Laney.

"The whole town is in an uproar about some strange light that lit up the whole village. That's why Tristan is here. Everyone's being questioned. They have both your parents now and know that you two have been missing."

"How is this possible? We weren't gone that long, were we?" Zeph asked, confused. *How had enough time passed for all this to happen?*

"What are we going to do, Zeph?" asked Laney, concerned. "Your mother. My parents."

Zeph began to feel panicked. He looked at Laney and then at Elbor, stunned and unsure of what to say.

Elbor's eyes shifted, quickly designing a plan in his head. "You two should stay out of sight for a while. There is nothing you can do for your families now. Follow me this way to my shop," Elbor offered. "I'll give you some luminai and enough food for a few days to get you out of here. I suggest you leave Adelaide for a while."

"Where will we go?" Laney wondered.

"I know someone who can help you."

Once they reached Elbor's store, he began loading a pack for them. "Go quickly northeast over the hills and keep going until you come to Rosten."

"You're sending us to Rosten?" Laney questioned. "We can't go there!"

"I know a man who owes me a debt," said Elbor. "Besides, Erikai would never suspect two young ones would ever go there on purpose. When you get there, find the trader known as Halleren.

You can trust him. When you find him, tell him I sent you, and show him this." Elbor pulled a black ring from among his things in the corner of the shop and placed it into Zeph's hand. "He will help keep you out of sight for now. I will come and find you when it's safe. If the snow keeps falling, it should cover your tracks behind you. I'll try and get word to your mother that you're all right, Zeph, and your parents, too, little lady," he said looking at Laney. "But I'll keep your whereabouts a secret."

Elbor placed his hand on Zeph's shoulder. "You take care of yourself, lad, and you watch over her, too."

"Thank you, Elbor," Zeph said, his feelings changing toward the old man. He trusted him more, enough to want to tell him about what had happened in the cave but decided against it.

"You'll need to avoid the gates," said Elbor. "I'm sure Tristan will have his guards and Shadow Men watching over them. Follow me to the east wall. I know of a small opening you should be able to squeeze through."

Zeph took Laney by the hand, Wiggin still clinging fast to her shoulder, as they followed Elbor out into the street and walked hurriedly in the opposite direction of the market square.

"If you want, I'll look after your noctambule for you. You don't want him making noise and giving you away," said Elbor as they approached the opening in the tall, stone wall.

"We'll be fine," replied Laney, and Wiggin agreed with a soft chirp.

"Please do whatever you can for . . . " said Zeph.

"I will," Elbor nodded in acknowledgement before Zeph and Laney disappeared through the narrow opening, wondering if they would ever see their new friend or their families again.

Chapter 6

The villagers were all moved into a large open area of the market square facing Tristan. The Shadow Men stood behind Zeph and Laney's parents with their heads hung low and faces stricken with worry.

Tristan shouted, "I am looking for a boy named Zephyr and a girl, Laney."

Elbor approached the crowd quietly and stood at the back, listening in.

"If you have seen them or know where they are," Tristan continued, "speak up now!"

The crowd fell silent as the people looked around at each other with suspicion. Tristan paused for a moment and then continued, "You must tell anything you know upon the command of the King, my father, Erikai." He paused. "If you speak now, you will be spared, but until they are found, your village will not receive any more luminai."

The crowd began to murmur as a few elderly villagers cautiously stepped forward and testified that they had witnessed the light coming from the south.

"Go!" Tristan commanded the Shadow Men, before turning to Zeph's mother and Laney's parents. His eyes studied them intently, but he did not say a word.

"Prince Tristan," whispered Zeph's mother. "Please . . . I know my son. He had nothing to do with this."

"Once we find him . . . and the girl," Tristan said as he turned his piercing gaze to Laney's parents, "then, we will learn if they are innocent or not."

"But they are just children, my Prince," said Laney's father, his voice trembling.

"The King, my father, wants everyone questioned, and your children so far are the only ones who are unaccounted for," Tristan said coldly.

He turned and left in the direction of the Shadow Men, following them south until they reached the foot of the caves. Tristan sent them to search through the caves, and after a long while, they returned to Tristan and reported, "There is no one here, Prince."

Tristan looked suspiciously at the Shadow Men, climbed up toward the cave, and walked past them. "Wait here," he said, grasping his luminai staff and stooping down to study the ground. He walked deeper inside until reaching the opening where Zeph and Laney had discovered the hidden path leading into the mysterious tomb.

A Shadow Man from the entrance to the cave yelled out to him, "There is nothing in there, Prince." Tristan turned, said nothing, and then stretched his luminai staff forward into the narrow crevice.

"What is this place?" Tristan muttered. His staff lit up most of the wide room, and he could see far enough down into the pit of skeleton bones into which Zeph had fallen.

As Tristan returned back to the entrance of the cave, the Shadow Men looked away, sensing his distrusting gaze.

"To my father," he said as he brushed past them.

King Erikai was waiting in his throne room when Prince Tristan arrived followed by the Shadow Men.

"Tristan!" Erikai said as he descended the steps to greet him. Tristan kneeled, and his father bent down and pulled him up. "Tell me, what news have you discovered in Adelaide, my son?"

"I have questioned everyone like you asked . . . except for a missing boy and girl. Their families are being guarded now, and I warned the other villagers not to get in the way."

"Do you think they have anything to do with this . . . light?" Erikai asked through gritted teeth.

"I don't know, Father," said Tristan before pausing.

"What is it, son? What else did you learn?" Erikai could tell there was more in Tristan's mind.

"Villagers said the light came from the south so I followed it to a group of caves. In one of them, I found a hidden path that led to an inner chamber. And there was a deep pit . . . what looked like an open grave."

Erikai was quiet for a moment. "Indeed," he said, his gaze shifting above Tristan into the distance.

"I believe that is where the light came from and has something to do with that room. Something tells me the two missing young ones are also involved somehow."

"That *is* intriguing," said Erikai, his eyes narrowing.

"You didn't know about it, did you?" Tristan asked, glancing to the right and left at the two Shadow Men standing on either side of him. They did not look at Tristan but kept their eyes fixed on Erikai.

"The tomb? Well, no, my son, I did not." Erikai answered, looking directly into Tristan's eyes. "However, it is important that we continue searching for these two young ones. Search out the other villages."

"My lord, we would be happy to find the boy and girl for you," said one of the Shadow Men, as if ignoring Tristan and moving in closer to stand in front of Erikai.

Erikai peered curiously at the Shadow Man standing before him and then to Tristan beyond whose brow tightened with annoyance.

"My son, you shall go, and take two Shadow Men with you," said Erikai after a long pause. "First, return to Adelaide and inquire of Elbor. Find out what he knows."

The Shadow Man's brow furrowed and its mouth curled with a sly grin at Tristan whose face remained unmoved.

"Very well, Father," Tristan said with a slight bow, and then he turned around and left, followed by the Shadow Men.

"Do you know where we're going, Zeph?" Laney asked after they had put some distance between them and Adelaide.

"Elbor said Rosten is northeast," he replied.

"What will we do when we get there?"

"Find this Halleren he mentioned, I guess."

"Are you sure we can trust him?"

"No, but I'm not sure we have much of a choice, Laney."

"Will we ever be able to return home? They will never stop until they find us."

Zeph did not respond for he knew Laney spoke the truth.

"And what about Adelaide? You know our village . . . our families will be forced to suffer on account of us!"

Zeph thought of his mother, and his heart grew heavy with concern. There was nothing he could do for her now, and she would want him to get as far away from Adelaide as possible. "We've already gone this far, Laney. We can't turn back now."

"But maybe if we went back and explained everything, the Prince would show us mercy?"

"Mercy?!" Zeph scoffed.

"Shh, wait!" whispered Laney suddenly. Wiggin's ears perked up and a low guttural sound moved up his throat.

"What is it?" Zeph wondered, swinging his torch around and pulling Laney by the hand in closer to himself.

"I thought I saw something . . . like someone or something just dashed by us."

Zeph peered long and hard toward the farthest edges of the illuminated area around them. He swept the torch once more around where they stood and gripped Laney's hand tightly.

"Maybe it's your mind playing tricks on you," he said. "I don't see or hear anything."

They continued walking for a long time, but with every step farther from home, Zeph felt less safe. He could not shake the feeling that they were being watched and followed, but he knew they could not find their way through the darkness without the light of the torch.

After several more miles, they both grew weary and decided to rest inside the opening of a shallow cave. Laney huddled closely with Wiggin curled up in her lap. She soon fell fast asleep against Zeph's shoulder. He struggled to stay awake to keep watch, but his eyes felt heavy and before long he, too, was sound asleep.

Zeph woke with a start to the sound of Laney's muffled yells and the feeling of a hot, sharp edge pressing firmly into his chest. His eyes focused in the glowing light of luminai as three masked figures encircled him.

"Who are you?" said the one who was holding the tip of his luminai staff at Zeph.

"Let her go!" Zeph yelled back, his eyes lit with fury. Another was holding Laney, his hand covering her mouth as she struggled to get free. A third was holding a sack that was shaking violently and muffling Wiggin's screeches.

"What do you want with us?" Zeph demanded. One of them approached Zeph and covered his head. Zeph felt the pressure of the staff release from his chest as he was yanked up to his feet.

Reacting quickly, Zeph thrust his elbow backward as hard as he could and took a blind swing with all of his might, his strike connecting with one of his captors who let out a loud groan. Zeph broke away, tore off the hood covering his head, and lunged toward the one holding Laney. A sharp blow to the back of his head, however, sent him sprawling to the ground and everything went black.

Chapter 7

Zeph awoke to Laney's echoing voice. As his eyes opened, he saw Wiggin sitting in her lap, licking Zeph's outstretched hand.

"Are you all right?" he said as he sat up slowly and embraced Laney.

"Yes, I'm fine," she replied, although he could tell her eyes held back tears.

Zeph turned to discover they were now in a much larger cavern. Across from him on the other side of a low burning fire sat an older man with long, grey hair and a thick beard slowly stirring a steaming pot. Beside him sat three other men with their masks removed, revealing their old and worn faces.

"What do you want with us?" Zeph sternly asked.

"You're a long way from home," the man said, not looking up at Zeph as he started to pour the stew into two bowls and then handed them over to the other men who carried them to Laney and Zeph.

"Have some. To be out this far you must be hungry."

Laney looked at Zeph with uncertainty. He hesitated for a moment, but then nodded, and they both began to eat.

"Sorry my men were rough with you when they found you. We aren't too careful when we come across something unusual out here. Tell me, what are two kids and a noctambule doing out here such a long way from any village?"

"My name's Zeph, and this is Laney. We're from Adelaide."

"Zeph. I heard of a Zeph from Adelaide once," the man said, startled. "You Daeron's kid?"

"You knew my father?" Zeph responded, leaning forward with widened eyes.

"I did. We're from Varkos, but I met your father long ago when we were rounded up by Erikai to work in the luminai mines, like the one you are sitting in right now," the man said, pointing around the cave with his spoon. "Erikai kept us all imprisoned at his palace before dispersing us. I never saw your father after those few days. He seemed like a good man, and I remember he spoke with a heavy heart of being separated from his wife and an infant son named Zeph."

"Could he still be alive?" Zeph pleaded.

"I don't know kid. Possible. He may have tried to escape like us. But chances are, if you never saw him again . . . " The man saw pain in Zeph's tense expression so he quickly changed the subject. "Now tell me, what brings the two of you out here all by yourselves?"

Zeph and Laney looked at each other. "We were on our way to Rosten," Zeph answered.

"Rosten!" the man scoffed. "What on earth has possessed you to go there? That awful place is a death sentence, especially for two young ones like you!"

"We got into some trouble, and a friend told us we could hide out with someone he trusts in Rosten."

The man looked around at the others as they shook their heads. "Are you certain you can trust this friend of yours?"

"My mother trusts him. He claims he knew my father. He sent us to Rosten with this." Zeph reached into his coat and pulled out the black ring that Elbor had given him, holding it out in the firelight for the man to see.

"Ah, the brotherhood. This friend, he wouldn't be a luminai trader, would he?" the man asked, continuing to eat.

Zeph nodded.

"I hate to break it to you, kid, but not all who possess that ring can be trusted. This belonged to the brotherhood of slaves who planned their escape to freedom from the mines. There were some, however, who betrayed us. One of them did this to me," he said as he leaned forward into the light to reveal a dark scar that ran from his eye down to his neck. "They got their own freedom by selling their souls to Erikai, and he made them luminai traders in the villages. I'm really sorry, kid. I know this is hard for you to hear. Now tell me, what kind of trouble would you two be in that would send you fleeing to Rosten?"

Zeph struggled to get the words out in his anger, knowing now that Elbor had deceived them, so Laney spoke up for him and told the whole story of the strange light, the arrival of Tristan in Adelaide, and how Elbor had helped them escape.

"By now, I imagine Elbor has already told Tristan where you two are going. Tell me, what do you two know about this world's past?"

"Not much, just rumors . . . legends," replied Zeph. "We know that no one is allowed to speak about it. But I have had recurring dreams . . ."

"Yeah? What kind of dreams?" It was the first time the man had looked Zeph directly in the eye.

"Well . . . the world is different. It's very bright and colorful and full of life. I know it's our world, but it looks nothing like it does now. The few stories I've heard is that our world once used to be like this but that Erikai somehow brought the darkness."

"You're not far off, kid. The secrets of our world have been kept from you young ones because Erikai wanted you to know nothing else . . . that you would never know what this world was like or that it could ever be that way again. The fact that you stumbled upon that cave gives me some hope. Somehow you two are important and need to stay safe."

"So, what should we do?" Laney wondered.

"The best thing to do now is take you to Mara."

"And where is Mara?"

"Mara's not a place. She's a person. She lives far out in the Bleak Mountains in isolation, but you'll be safe with her. Erikai knows nothing of her, and you can trust her. Get some rest, and we'll set out in a few hours. We can't remain here long, because I am sure Tristan isn't far behind you."

"Before we can trust you, I need to ask you something," said Zeph.

"I don't think you have much of a choice, kid, but go ahead. And the name is Dylan."

"Why hasn't anyone done anything about Erikai? There are more of us in this world than him."

"That sounds like treasonous talk . . . It's the Shadow Men I'm afraid," Dylan continued. "We're helpless against them. So instead, we've made war on each other to survive. Besides, Zeph, people have to believe that change is possible and that others will join with them before they will stand up and act. Who's going to be the first one to stick his—or her—neck out first?" he said, glancing at Zeph and then Laney. "Yeah, maybe you two would be crazy enough, but you're young and still got a lot to learn. Now try and get a few hours' rest. It's a hard journey to Mara, and we'll leave soon."

"Won't you tell us more?" Laney asked.

"Soon, but not now. Get some rest."

Zeph and Laney both had trouble falling asleep, their thoughts spinning with all that they had heard. Was there anyone left in the world beside each other they could trust?

"Prince Tristan!" said Elbor with a bow. "I'm honored by your presence. To what do I owe the pleasure of your—"

"Drop the show, Elbor," Tristan interrupted, pacing around the small, candlelit shop. He picked up a small round object from a shelf and began turning it around in the palm of his hand. "The two young ones that have gone missing from the village. What do you know about them?"

"I'm not sure what you are talking about."

"Liar!" yelled out a Shadow Man as it swiftly glided up in front of him. Its large, dark figure knocked past shelves and sent objects falling to the floor, and it towered over Elbor. "I can s-s-s-s-smell the fear in you! What are you hiding?"

"Not a thing," Elbor answered, trying to hide his disgust and fear.

"Shall I force it out of him, Prince?" the Shadow Man asked, as it glided a bony finger along Elbor's throat.

Tristan confidently sauntered over and pushed his way in front of the Shadow Man, ignoring its question. "How long has it been, Elbor, since my father gave you your freedom? He made you a trader of luminai, and in return he expects your cooperation—to be his eyes and ears with all that goes on in this village. That was his agreement. You must know more. You are not telling us everything."

"Well, then, my Prince." Elbor's countenance and voice suddenly changed, trying to appear confident. "I will tell you, but first I'd like the promise of an increase in my supply of luminai to trade and double the share of its profits."

"He's trembling, Prince," said a Shadow Man mockingly as it began to move about the shop, extinguishing all the candlelight with its fingers, leaving only the hot glow of Tristan's luminai staff which he began to press up against Elbor's neck.

"Of course he is. Elbor knows better than to bargain with the son of the King. Who are they? Just tell me what you know!" Tristan's voice became fiercer and the tip of his staff pressed in harder.

"Rosten," Elbor struggled to say.

"Rosten! Don't take me for a fool, Elbor! Two young ones wouldn't survive an hour there," Tristan said as he backed away.

"I sent them to Halleren, the trader . . . with my ring."

"Ah yes, the brotherhood. You still have the ring even though you betrayed them long ago," said Tristan. "So you persuaded them to go to Rosten and thought you might use that to bargain with me, is that it?"

Elbor looked down and away but felt Tristan's icy stare.

"We leave for Rosten, then, and if I don't find them there, you can be sure I'll be back to see you."

Chapter 8

"Come, it's time to leave," said Dylan, shaking Zeph awake. "We have quite a way to go before we reach Mara." Dylan and the three other men began putting out the fire and busily packed up their things.

Wiggin perched happily on Laney's arm and ate out of her hand.

"How did you find him?" Dylan asked her, crouching down and holding out his hand to scratch behind Wiggin's soft, furry ear-wings. "There aren't many of his kind left. They are great survivors," he said as he stood back up to his feet, "but most of them have been hunted. They normally don't trust people."

"I found him alone," she said as Wiggin took another bite. "He was injured. I took care of him, tamed him. He's been loyal to me ever since."

"Dylan, let's get going," said one of his men.

"Well, he's a good friend to have." Dylan smiled at Laney. They lit their four luminai staffs and started walking through the hills. Dylan and another man walked in front, with Zeph and Laney in between followed by the other two.

"So tell us more about Mara," Zeph called out after they had walked a while in silence.

"She's a rather strange old woman," Dylan answered. "She doesn't talk . . . or can't."

"Can't?" Laney wondered.

"Yes, been that way as long as we've known her," Dylan answered.

"And how long is that?" Zeph asked.

"When we escaped from the mines long ago, we fled to the Bleak Mountains where we met Mara. She was kind to give us food and shelter. They never found us, and Erikai spread the word that escaped slaves from each of the villages had been killed for treason. Mara is among the few who knows that we are still alive. We were actually on our way to see her after getting some supplies in Varkos when we found you."

"Don't you have families? Did you never see them again?" Laney asked.

"Emrick here was the only one with a family," said Dylan as he grasped the shoulder of the man walking next to him. "A wife and a son. She didn't believe the rumors of Emrick's death, and she went out with the boy looking for him. We have never found them and don't know what ever happened to them."

"I'm sorry," Laney said sympathetically, but Emrick did not respond.

"I believe it's time you kids learn the truth about this world," said Dylan. "This place wasn't always like it is now. You would have to see it to believe it. It was incredible. So much light and color. There was life all around, and the world was at peace. No war. No poverty. No have and have-nots. It all began with the light creators. They were the first to bring the world to life out of darkness. Their beautiful songs created light and made the world come alive. Then many of them were married and had children who inherited their abilities. When I was young there were probably a dozen light creators just in Varkos."

"What happened to them?" Zeph asked with wonder.

"Erikai happened. He killed them all off one by one. You see, there was no king in our world before Erikai. The light creators weren't really sovereigns. They had the power to create light and give life to the world, but everything was fair and just and good. When the age of darkness began, that is when this world became what it is now—the injustice, the violence, the fear."

"And luminai?" Zeph started to ask.

"Yes, the voices of the light creators activated the natural energy in the luminai. Boy, I wish you could have heard the haunting melody of their voices all over this land. It was the most beautiful thing you ever heard. Sometimes you would forget it was even there because it just seemed to move in and with and through and around everything else—like the whole world was breathing."

"Those bodies we found in the caves . . . " Laney muttered.

"Maybe a tomb of light creators," Dylan responded. "Erikai must have thought he had hidden it forever, but you two found it searching for your noctambule. The strange light event that you spoke about in the cave. It must have come from the bones you fell on, Zeph."

"And there are no light creators left?" Laney asked.

"None. All gone. Erikai wanted control, and he believed the only way to have it was to kill them off. All of them. Then, with his Shadow Men he took control and was even able to lure men from the villages to his side."

"Like Elbor," Zeph said, kicking at the ground.

"Elbor started as a slave in the mines with us. With the light creators gone, the luminai had to be mined and heated another way, and Erikai wanted control of that as well. Several of us started a brotherhood determined to escape and get luminai to our people free of Erikai. But as Erikai began to give certain men more freedom, more authority, he made bargains with them, and they succumbed."

"I don't understand."

"It's called power and compromise, Zeph, even when that power is given by someone as evil and hated as Erikai. He was sly in the way he did it, too. The more authority he gave them, the more he won over their favor. Like Elbor, they began to see the rest of us as their enemies, too. And they were afraid to lose what they possessed."

"So they betrayed the brotherhood," Zeph responded.

Dylan was quiet and then sighed, "Yes."

"And the Shadow Men . . . who . . . what are they, and where did they come from? They aren't like us at all," Laney added with a tremor in her voice.

"No one really knows, but stories say they are connected in some way to magic from our world's past age, before the light creators. That's all we really know about them."

"Can they be defeated?" Zeph wondered.

"I don't know. They are extremely fast and strong. They thrive in the darkness, and some have even said they can take the shape of anything they see . . . including us."

With that revelation Laney and Zeph fell into fearful silence until all that could be heard was the sound of their steps along the ground.

After a long pause Dylan stated, "As you can see, there's not much hope for this world, but what happened to you back in that cave . . . I haven't heard of anything like that before."

They walked along a high ridge for several more miles. Zeph and Laney thought of how quickly their lives had changed, but they were glad they were together. They felt like they could trust Dylan, but they knew they had both been wrong about Elbor, too.

Far away in the distance they began to see a valley full of dim flickers of light.

"Down over there, that's Rosten," said Dylan. "Our path takes us far around there. We won't even get close. They have scouts and deigrods lurking about in the hills nearby."

"Deigrods? I've never seen one up close!" Zeph exclaimed.

"That's because there's not many left in the world . . . either killed for food or made into weapons by Rosten. They were once peaceful creatures but became more vicious in the age of darkness when they became prey to hunters."

"And you better hope you never encounter one," interjected Emrick who had not yet spoken a word.

"Speaking of which," Dylan said, pulling a sharp, twin-bladed knife from his belt and handing it to Zeph. "You'll need this."

"What about me?" Laney asked.

"Well, you have your noctambule, and, honestly, I'd rather have him at my side," Dylan said with a chuckle.

As Dylan had said, their path took them out of sight of Rosten, which pleased both Laney and Zeph. They were glad that Dylan and his men had found them before they had ever reached the village.

Several more hours passed by, and they walked for miles over rocky hills and through desolate forests and valleys.

"We're getting close," said Dylan, noticing that Zeph and Laney's pace was beginning to slow and they looked tired. A strong wind was starting to blow against them.

Suddenly, Wiggin's earwings perked up as he turned his head abruptly and pointed his furry face toward the sky. A low growl began to sound in his throat.

"Wiggin, what is it?!" Laney asked, feeling the talons on his feet dig a little stronger into her shoulder. "He senses something nearby," Laney said, turning to Dylan.

"Get behind us!" insisted Dylan, as he and the other men instantly formed a circle around Zeph and Laney. They gripped their luminai staffs tightly and pointed them back up the hill in the direction from which they had just descended. Zeph saw Dylan pull something out from his belt and fling it quickly down by his side. A sharp, metal sound pierced the silence as a long silver blade shot out instantly.

All was quiet except for the hum of the wind. Laney tried to hush Wiggin who sat trembling on her shoulder. She moved in closer to Zeph, his heart beating fast and his fist tightly clutching the knife given to him by Dylan in his right hand. Everything was still in the glow of luminai, but beyond the rim of light was darkness.

"Could it be a scout?" Emrick whispered to Dylan.

"Not likely, not this far out from Rosten," he replied as he inched closer to the edge of the darkness, his eyes squinting and his ears listening intently.

Suddenly, a large creature burst into the light from the darkness with a fierce roar and swung at Dylan, knocking him to the ground. Before the other men could react, the ferocious deigrod lunged toward them, flinging them aside effortlessly with a powerful swing of his head. Laney and Zeph quickly darted away as the sound of a spear whizzed past their heads and they tumbled down a hill.

"Wiggin!" Laney cried out, sensing that he was no longer with them. She looked back through the flashes of light to see Wiggin attacking a rider on top of the deigrod. There was a loud yell and then the sound of a body falling onto the ground. Emrick and the other men were back on their feet and jabbing at the deigrod aggressively with their luminai staffs while Dylan thrust his long, sharp weapon repeatedly into the back of the beast's neck. The deigrod roared out in pain and swept them all back again, sliding across the snowy ground.

Laney called out after Zeph as he gripped his knife and ran back up the hill toward the fallen rider who was still wrestling on the ground with Wiggin biting at his neck. As Zeph drew nearer, Wiggin was thrown through the air. The rider laying on his back kicked Zeph hard in the chest with both feet sending him sprawling backwards.

Emrick quickly jumped on the rider and pinned him down. The others roped the deigrod's flailing neck as Dylan continued to stab at the beast until at last it slowly crumpled to the ground in a heap. Dylan pulled his blade out from the deigrod's flesh and fell exhausted to his knees.

Laney helped Zeph to his feet. Wiggin settled back on her shoulder as she and Zeph rushed over to gaze up on the mysterious creature. The deigrod's long, strong legs and wide paws sprawled out, his tongue fell loosely out of his large gaping mouth full of teeth sharp as daggers, and his hairy, black and red striped side heaved up and down slowly with each struggling and misty breath.

Dylan approached and knelt beside Emrick, with the rider still pinned down on his back.

"Who are you?" Dylan inquired angrily, still breathing heavily and grasping the stranger from behind his neck, which was cut and bleeding from Wiggin's attack. The man's face was hidden beneath a head of long, black hair and a thick beard. "You're a scout from Rosten, aren't you?!"

"Yes!" the man responded with a grunt.

"Since when do scouts ever come out this far?"

"The light of your luminai on the ridge. I saw it and followed you."

"Are you alone?" Emrick demanded.

"Yes, otherwise you'd all be dead," he taunted.

"We should kill him, Dylan!" Emrick insisted.

"We should, and in different circumstances we would have," Dylan answered back, peering back at Laney and Zeph who were both still in shock from all that happened. "Get him up, we need to keep moving."

"What about the deigrod?" Laney said with concern as she looked into the animal's sad eyes. It breathed slower and heavier now, and its fierce anger had subsided.

"There's nothing we can do now. He'll be dead soon. I'm afraid it is kill or be killed with these creatures since Rosten turned the last of their kind into weapons. They keep them locked up, torture them, and sometimes even have them fight for sport. Probably breeding them, too. I don't believe you two would have even made it to Rosten alive."

The scout began to laugh. "Rosten? The young ones were going to Rosten?"

"We were on our way to find a man named Halleren," Zeph said. "Do you know him?"

"Halleren, the trader? What on earth for?"

Dylan interrupted, "Why don't you tell us why you attacked us? We weren't anywhere near Rosten."

"Like I said, I spotted your light way up on the ridge," the scout replied sounding irritated. "I was afraid I'd lose sight of you if I went back to tell the others. Then, when my deigrod sniffed out your noctambule . . . well, let's just say we haven't seen one of those in a long time either." Wiggin growled and licked his teeth as the scout peered at him with interest. "I reckon that is what my deigrod was really after. Although, he would have enjoyed devouring all of you if he had the chance!"

"So these creatures you abuse really mean nothing to you then?" Laney demanded.

"Besides for food and for killing?" He grinned.

"That's enough! Tie him up, blindfold him, and gag him," Dylan said as he shoved the scout toward Emrick, to whom he muttered, "I promise as soon as we leave the young ones behind, we'll deal with him then."

After hiking on for several more hours, they finally reached the summit of a much steeper mountain range, and Dylan moved aside some timber that had been covering a narrow opening leading into a tunnel in the mountain.

"We're almost there now," Dylan said. "There is a valley on the other side of this mountain. Wait here and keep a watch over our new friend." He motioned to the other two men.

One of the men grabbed the scout roughly by the neck and shoved him down harshly against a large, heavy stone. He mumbled something imperceptible through his gag, but neither of the men responded.

Dylan glared at the scout before turning to the two men again, "We'll be back soon." Zeph and Laney stepped through the opening and followed Dylan with Emrick into the mountain.

Chapter 9

Laney and Zeph grew more anxious to meet Mara as Dylan led them through the long, narrow tunnel. "Remember, Mara can't speak, but she can hear and understand you," he told them. "She is one of the few people left in this world that I trust. You will be safe with her."

"How has Erikai never known of her living here?" asked Laney.

"He never found the opening or the tunnel that leads through it to the valley. Ah, and here we are."

They reached the end and walked out into a vast, open space. The air was still and much warmer, and the sound of gentle, rolling waves filled the silence. The light of Dylan and Emrick's luminai staffs only reached to the edge of the shoreline down a shallow slope before disappearing into the thick darkness. A long, wooden boat sat resting on the shore.

"You can't see her home from here. This boat is the only way to get across to the other side," Dylan said as he led their way down to it. After Zeph and Laney had climbed in, Dylan and Emrick shoved off into the open water and started rowing, one standing at each end of the boat. Laney reached out her hand to touch the water, which looked like beautiful dark blue glass under the glow of the luminai staffs she and Zeph were holding. "It feels warm," she said, surprised.

"This valley is surrounded by an enclosed wall of mountains," answered Dylan, "and luminai is plentiful here and keeps this whole area warmer than anywhere else. Mara gets her own luminai now from the bottom of the lake with a device we helped her build. This lake is also teeming with creatures you won't see anywhere else in this world. You may see one or two on our way."

Sure enough, several long, slithering creatures with transparent, bright wings came up to the surface. They bobbed their heads and drifted through the dark blue water alongside the boat. Zeph and Laney were speechless. They had not seen creatures like this before.

"It's like something I've seen in a dream," Laney said. Wiggin eyed them curiously and licked his chops hungrily.

"Did you hear that?" Laney suddenly asked, looking all around her in surprise.

"Hear what?" Zeph replied.

"A woman's voice. It was soft but clear . . . as if she was with us in the boat. She said, 'You've come a long way.'"

"I didn't hear anything," Dylan answered. "Are you sure?"

"There it is again. She said, 'I knew one day you'd come.'"

"Look!" Zeph pointed past Dylan who was standing at the front of the boat. They could see a small but growing light in the distance as they moved closer.

"That's Mara's home," said Dylan.

Laney's heart raced. After a long pause, she cried out, "The voice is Mara's!"

"How do you know, Laney?" Zeph wondered.

"Because she just told me," Laney answered, stunned. Then Wiggin gave a loud yelp as she suddenly dropped the luminai staff and slumped over.

Zeph put down his own staff and grabbed her by the shoulders. "Laney!" he yelled, but she didn't move. "Laney! Dylan, she won't answer me! What's wrong with her?"

Laney's mouth began to move and form words but made no sound. The light toward which they were rowing got brighter and larger until they arrived at the opposite shore of the lake and could see a small, simple cottage lit up from the inside.

Zeph spotted a short, bare-footed woman with long, grey hair standing in a tattered gown waiting at the edge of the shore and holding a lantern.

Emrick tossed her a rope, and she pulled the boat in toward the shore. "Mara," Dylan said, embracing her as he stepped out from the boat. She quickly released him and went straight to Laney who still lay unconscious in Zeph's arms. Zeph looked up at Mara and tightened his grip protectively on Laney, but Mara did not even seem to notice him. Her face was coarse and aged, but her eyes were wide with intensity. She grasped Laney and frantically began to pull her away from Zeph out of the boat. Zeph instinctively clutched Laney and would not let her go, but he felt a tight squeeze on his shoulder, holding him back. He spun around, his eyes ablaze with fury and desperation, prepared to shout at whoever was restraining him.

"She's trying to help, Zeph," Emrick calmly reassured him, and behind his own fear, Zeph could make out a hopefulness in Emrick's eyes that told Zeph he could trust Mara.

Zeph sighed and hesitantly helped to lift Laney out from the boat, but he kept a firm grip on her as they carried her inside the cottage and laid her down on Mara's bed.

"What's wrong with her?!" Zeph asked, never taking his eyes off of Laney's still form. Mara made no sound. She held Laney's hand and gently stroked her face. Tears streamed down her cheeks as she pressed her forehead against Laney's. Wiggin remained curled up beside her, trying to nudge her awake.

All of a sudden, Laney sat up with a start. "Tristan!" she yelled out. Mara gasped, and Wiggin shot up into the air, his tail wagging swiftly back and forth happily above her.

"Laney!" Zeph exclaimed, relieved. She turned and looked at Zeph but it was a few moments before she fully regained consciousness and recognized him.

"You're all right. You're safe," Zeph reassured her as he wrapped his arms around her and rubbed her back comfortingly.

"What happened? Where are we?" she asked, bewildered.

Dylan placed his hand on Mara's trembling shoulder. "We're in Mara's home now," he said as he dropped his bag onto a chair while Emrick knelt down in front of a pot cooking over a crackling fire.

Mara had stepped back when Laney awoke, but she continued to look at her with astonishment.

"She's speaking to me. Can no one else hear her?" Laney wondered, as she looked around at the others. "I'm Laney," she said, turning back to Mara. "This is Zeph. We're from Adelaide. Dylan found us and brought us here. He said we'd be safe here . . . with you."

"It's Prince Tristan whom they're seeking refuge from, Mara," Dylan added. Mara immediately turned to him upon hearing that name, and her eyes widened and then became somber. "He's been chasing after them. They were told by someone they trusted to hide out in Rosten, but we came across them just in time. You'll be very interested to hear their story, old friend."

"She says she's been waiting for this day for a long time," Laney said to the others. "What does that mean? You've been waiting for *me*?" She looked at Mara curiously.

The room was quiet. Mara's eyes fixed on Laney, and she slowly approached her again, grabbed her by the hand, and sat down beside her on the bed.

"What is she saying?" Zeph insisted.

"She says she saw us while we were in the boat on the lake. Not with her eyes, but with her mind. That voice I heard in my head was hers." Laney's wide eyes moved back and forth between looking at the others and staring intently at Mara. She held Laney's young cheek delicately in her old, weathered hand and a smile that had been tested by years of isolation yet still held a touch of gentleness, played across her lips. "She says . . . she says she was a light creator."

"What?" Zeph said, startled.

"Mara, a light creator?" Dylan asked in disbelief. "Not possible. They all died. That tomb you found . . . "

"She says Erikai did this to her long ago," Laney said looking at Dylan and then back to Mara, her eyes softening. Mara pulled her greasy gray hair back over one shoulder and lifted her neck to reveal in the dim light a long, thin blackened scar that ran across the top of her throat. "She says that Erikai killed all the light creators to seize power. Except for her. The Shadow Men did this to her, removing the use of her voice. Go on," Laney said to her tenderly.

It became quiet again. Mara's weeping face hung down as Laney repeated to the others all that Mara was saying to her. "She says her name is not Mara but actually Naomi. After they did this to her, they cast her out. She was treated like an outcast by everyone, so people began to call her Mara. She says she found this to be a place of solitude within the mountains and has been living here ever since."

"Does Erikai know that you're alive?" Zeph asked her.

"Yes," Laney answered for her. "But he doesn't know where she is hiding or that she is known as Mara now."

"Why didn't you ever try and communicate this to me? Didn't you trust me, old friend?" Dylan asked, shaking his furrowed brow.

"She says she has been waiting for the day when her hopes would be answered, and now that time has come. With me," Laney answered.

"How is Laney the only one able to hear you?" Zeph asked Naomi.

Naomi looked up at Laney who sat up straight suddenly and leaned back away from her with her eyes widening in shock. Pulling her hand away from Naomi, she looked first at Dylan and then at Zeph. "No! That can't be!"

"What? What did she say?" Zeph asked with a tone of distrust.

"She says the only way is that I must be a light creator, too."

"What? How—how can that be? Your parents, they're—they're not . . . " Zeph stuttered, unable to control his racing thoughts.

Laney stood up, visibly shaking and backing slowly away from Naomi. "It's impossible. How is this true?" she asked, her mind swirling with doubt.

Naomi stood up to approach Laney, but Laney held out the palm of one hand while trying to steady herself on Zeph with the other. After a few moments, Laney said, "It's not my parents, Zeph. She says it must be a pure connection to luminai—the way it was for the very first light creators. "

Zeph sat quietly, contemplating this revelation. "So Laney could be the one to bring our world out of darkness," he finally stated, growing more and more eager.

"What are you saying, Zeph? I don't know how to create light."

"Naomi could show you. Won't you?" Zeph answered, turning to Naomi who nodded hesitantly. "You have to. You're the only hope for this world we have left."

"No, she says we're not." Laney said, looking questioningly at Naomi, and then she suddenly gasped in horror. "No!"

"Who? Who is it, Laney?" Zeph called out impatiently to her.

"I don't believe it, Zeph, and neither will you," she answered before pausing and continuing in a shocked tone. "Prince Tristan."

Through Laney, Naomi went on to explain the story of how long ago she had fallen in love with Erikai but that the other light creators had urged against it, not trusting him. In her devotion to him, she ignored their warnings and left them. They were married and had a child—Tristan. Not long after he was born, Erikai created the Shadow Men and killed off all of the light creators and their children, except for Naomi, whom he exiled, and their son Tristan.

"Tristan doesn't know he is a light creator, and he doesn't know what really happened to his mother—to Naomi. How much pain you have had to carry alone all these years!" Laney expressed to Naomi with sorrow in her eyes. Her heart broke for this old woman sitting before her now whose husband had long ago betrayed her and whose son knew nothing of her existence. Her growing hatred toward Erikai and the estrangement from her son over the years had been buried deep within her. She had, long ago, given up any hope for her own life and only longed for the day when another light creator would ascend and the age of light would return.

"All this time, I had no idea," Dylan said, shaking his head.

"We must stop Erikai!" Zeph said emphatically.

"Like I said before, kid, the Shadow Men can't be stopped," Dylan answered him. "If Erikai finds out about Laney, he will definitely kill her too."

"She says they can be defeated!" Laney abruptly remarked, standing up to her feet next to Naomi.

"How?" Dylan asked incredulously as they all turned to look at Laney.

"Tristan. She says Tristan alone can kill the Shadow Men. Erikai created them from Tristan's life blood using ancient magic. They are Tristan, but only a part of him. She says only he can destroy them."

"Then Prince Tristan needs to know the truth!" Zeph bellowed.

"He'll never listen to us," Dylan answered. "We're his enemies. Anyways, he's loyal to his father and he's devoted to keeping this world in darkness."

"The truth will change that. Once Tristan realizes—"

"It's too late, Zeph. Tristan's heart is far too consumed by hate to ever see the truth," Dylan responded. "I'm sorry, my friend," he said sympathetically and looked toward Naomi.

"He's right," Emrick chimed in. "Tristan is beyond salvation. He has too much blood on his hands."

"Then what are we going to do?" Laney demanded. "We can't hide here forever. We have family who need us. Aren't you tired of living like this? All of this, finding the tomb, meeting Naomi, must have happened for a reason. Can't you see that?"

"These are strange occurrences indeed, young one, and for a moment I believed maybe . . . but you are still just kids. I wish I had the hope you do," Dylan answered. "But I've lived a lot longer than you have, and I have seen evil you cannot even begin to imagine. Come, Emrick, it is time we go. I promise we will return in a few days, but for now I urge you to stay with Mar—Naomi. Sorry that's going to take some getting used to, old friend," he said, putting his arm around Naomi and kissing her on the forehead.

Emrick and Dylan packed up some food and luminai and launched the long boat back out into the darkness. "We'll be back soon. We have some unfinished business to take care of on the other side of the mountain," Dylan said, referring to the scout from Rosten. "You all take this time and get to know each other more." He smiled back at them.

Dylan and Emrick made their way back through the mountain but as they approached the other opening they noticed that there was no light waiting for them at the entrance. As they came out of the mouth of the tunnel, they turned and saw the two other men lying on the ground. Dylan let out a strangled cry as Emrick knelt down and placed his hand on their chests.

"Dead, both of them, Dylan."

The scout had somehow loosened his bonds and overpowered the two men, slitting both of their throats and escaping with their luminai.

"We should have killed him when we had the chance!" Emrick said bitterly.

Dylan struck his luminai staff hard against the ground in anger. "He's gone, Emrick. Probably on his way back to Rosten."

"Their blood is still warm, Dylan! This did not happen that long ago. If we hurry we may still be able to reach him before he gets there."

"Yes, let's go," Dylan agreed, his expression darkening. "That scout knows too much, and if he talks, this mountain won't be a safe place anymore."

Chapter 10

Prince Tristan and the Shadow Men descended the hill toward Rosten. Two scout riders came lunging out from the gate towards them on deigrods but immediately reared back when they saw it was the Prince.

"Prince Tristan!" one of them stated, startled by their royal visitors. "What is the honor of . . . We thought you were . . . "

"Who? You thought I was who?" Tristan inquired with a deadly demeanor.

A—a scout who has been missing!" The scout stuttered. "We've been expecting his return. We saw your light coming closer and thought it might be him."

"I'm here to see your trader named Halleren," Tristan answered coldly. "You will take me to him."

"Right away, my Prince," one of the scout riders answered nervously.

The town of Rosten was active when Tristan walked through the gate. People stopped what they were doing and bowed as their Prince passed by. Children clung to their mothers and eyed Tristan timidly.

The town of Rosten was the poorest of the villages, and the haze and odor of root weed smoke was everywhere. Along the way, they passed several large deigrod cages. In one of them, a roaring deigrod was being stabbed at and whipped. The deigrod lunged at the cage as Tristan walked by. He turned and looked into the animal's fierce eyes and could feel the deigrod's misty breath as it licked its sharp teeth. Their gaze met for a brief moment before the sharp sting of the whip sent the deigrod spinning around again. Tristan tensed with a strange sense of pity for the creature which he quickly dismissed.

Down pathways through crowded streets and barrel fires, Tristan followed the scout rider to the open market area as he announced the Prince's arrival and the people either bowed or slowly scattered away. Surrounding the market were a dozen dingy trading shacks. Underneath an overhang protruding from one of the shops, several men were sitting and drinking at long tables, but as soon as Prince Tristan and the Shadow Men approached, they got up, took their drinks, and left quickly. That is, except for two rather large men who were passed out on the table.

The scout rider approached one of the shops and called out for Halleren. Tristan roughly kicked the table in front of him where the two unconscious men lay. One of the men immediately sat upright. His greasy reddish hair was tousled over his face, and his mouth was slobbery with foam from his drink.

"Hey! Whudya want?" he said with slurred speech. The man stood up, half stumbling toward Tristan. He was a few heads taller with broad shoulders. "Whodya think you are?"

"Bow, you ignorant fool!" replied a Shadow Man. "This is the son of King Erikai, your Prince."

"Ohhhh, Prince Tristan, eh?" the large man said, spitting the foam from his mouth and giving a clumsy bow toward Tristan.

The Shadow Man lunged at the heckler with a low snarl, but Tristan quickly thrust out his luminai staff to hold it back.

"You don't care who I am?" Tristan asked curiously, gently lowering his staff, looking with confidence into the man's face as he moved in closer.

"Should I?"

"You're not afraid of me then?"

By now, the other man at the table had also stood up. Out of the corner of his eye, Tristan noticed him grab a sharp object from the table and hold it behind his back.

"You . . . your father . . . you ain't nothin' without your Shadow Men," said the man standing in front of Tristan and whose breath reeked of liquor. "One of these days, this world won't belong to you no more!"

"Is that right?" Tristan demanded. "Do you know what my father does to people who talk like that?"

The large man hesitated for a moment and then took a wide swing. Tristan easily dodged it, and in a manner of seconds swiftly kicked the man just above the knee before jabbing the end of his luminai staff into the man's abdomen and shoving his head down onto the table.

The large man toppled over backward onto the ground, and before the second man could react, Tristan had already leapt over the table toward him. The man swung a knife at Tristan, but Tristan swung his cloak out in front of him to defend the attack, spun around, and struck the back of the man's head with his luminai staff. The man reeled forward in pain and turned back to face Tristan at the very moment the end of his staff was swinging rapidly upward, connecting solidly with the man's jaw and sending him sprawling backward onto the table.

By this time the first man was up again and charging at Tristan who had his back turned, but before he could reach him, a Shadow Man clasped the man by the neck tightly. The man fell at once to his knees, his face turning pale as he gasped for air. Tristan held up his hand, and the Shadow Man dropped the limp man onto the ground with a reluctant growl.

"Prince Tristan!" Halleren said as he stepped out cautiously into view from the darkness of his shop. "I apologize for these miscreants. To what do I owe your visit?" He bowed slightly, not averting his gaze from Tristan.

"I'm looking for two young ones who came here from Adelaide," said Tristan calmly as if unfazed.

"I don't know what you are referring to, my Prince," Halleren replied looking decidedly perplexed, eyeing warily the two fallen men out of the corner of his eye. "We've had no such visitors here. And I'm not sure they would have made it past our deigrods if they had tried."

Tristan narrowed his eyes and then repeated with growing impatience, "I'm looking for two young ones, a boy and a girl. Elbor told me he sent them here."

Halleren's voice began to slightly crack and his body started to tremble. "I promise you, Prince. I know nothing about this. Why on earth would he send them to me?"

"Either you're lying," answered Tristan, "or Elbor's lying. Now where are they?"

One of the Shadow Men crept toward Halleren and grabbed him by the collar of his coat, dragging him effortlessly toward Tristan and pushing him down on his knees in front of him.

"Tell your Prince the truth," hissed the Shadow Man as it reached forward to strangle Halleren, but before it could do so, Tristan lifted his hand. "Leave us, and go wait at the gate."

"Prince?" The Shadow Man's gaze narrowed in surprise.

"Both of you," Tristan said, staring coldly at them until both Shadow Men, scowling, turned and left.

Tristan slowly pulled Halleren up to his feet.

"Bring me a drink," he said calmly.

Halleren stumbled in confusion back into the shack as Tristan stepped over one of the fallen men and sat down at the table. A few minutes later Halleren came back with a mug foaming to the brim that he placed in front of Tristan.

"Sit down," Tristan said nodding at the open seat across the table.

Halleren sat down, his eyes locked on Tristan as he pulled back his hood.

"My, Prince. I promise you. I know nothing of any young ones visiting here."

"My father supplies you with the luminai for trading and lets you keep more than your share. You, Elbor—you were mine slaves once, but my father freed you and put you where you are. Elbor tried to barter with me. Don't even think of trying to do the same. You think because Rosten has been training deigrods that you are strong? Maybe you think your pitiful village is even becoming more powerful than my father?"

"Never, Prince. I promise. Look around. We're destitute, and we remain loyal to our king. And to you."

"Then tell me. The young ones. Where are they?"

"Maybe they are lost in the wilderness. Maybe they decided to go to Varkos. You know it would be crazy for young ones to try and come here. I even fear for my own life. It's only my position as a trader that protects me."

"Maybe you're right. And maybe I'll deal with Elbor later. Until then, I'll just stay here and wait."

After a few moments of awkward silence, Halleren could tell that Tristan wanted to be alone, so he slowly rose up and went back inside the shack. The once busy marketplace was now eerily quiet except for the sound of a few voices, crackling fire barrels, and the creaking of old timber shacks in the wind.

Out of the corner of his eye, Tristan noticed a small boy in dirty clothes, about five years old, inching closer to him.

Tristan turned to face him, raising his eyebrow. "What is it, boy? What do you want?"

The boy stood silently. He had a furry round cap on his head and his shaggy hair fell over his soft blue eyes. His face was covered with dirt and ash.

"Do you know who I am?" Tristan asked, but the boy remained silent. "Where's your mother? Does she know you are out here by yourself?"

A small smile peeked out on the boy's somber face.

"You know, I was your age once. That's when I learned to use one of these," Tristan said as he pulled out a long blade. "Here, you hold it." Tristan handed it to the boy who took it without hesitation, and his smile grew larger.

"Liam! Liam!" came a desperate woman's voice. The young boy quickly handed the blade back to Tristan and turned to see his mother running towards him.

"I'm so sorry, my Prince. I beg you. He's too young. He doesn't know." She bowed to him without looking him in the eye.

"I'd keep a better watch over your son, woman," Tristan responded. "I dare say, he's quite a fearless one."

"Just like his father was," she said sheepishly as her eyes met Tristan's for a brief moment and then darted away. Tristan noticed that the woman was quite beautiful if not for the layers of dirt and dust that had accumulated on her face.

"Come along, Liam. I am truly sorry, my Prince," she said as she pulled the young boy along. He continued to peer back intrigued by Tristan who remained seated at the table and sharpening his blade.

"I thought I told you to wait for me," Tristan said some time later as he saw the two Shadow Men approaching, but he was surprised to see them dragging along someone else.

"And who is this?"

"The missing scout, Prince. Says he was captured by several men who were traveling with two young ones—a boy and girl!"

Tristan stood up immediately. "Where?" he asked, walking intently over toward the scout who began to cower. "Speak up!" Tristan yelled, grasping him by the jaw.

"They killed my deigrod. Had me blindfolded and gagged, but I escaped," the scout stuttered, avoiding Tristan's intense stare.

"Just tell me where!"

"Near the Bleak Mountains. I killed two of the men at the foot of the mountains, but there were two others with the young ones. They entered a hidden passage into the mountains . . . spoke of an old woman who lived on the other side."

"You'll take us back there now—with no deigrod," Tristan commanded the scout. "One of you will stay behind. The other one comes with me and this scout to the mountain," he said to the Shadow Men. "We'll leave immediately."

"And what of these rebels?" asked one of the Shadow Men looking toward the two fallen men overpowered by Tristan and still laid out cold. "Are they to be left unpunished? If word of this spreads . . . or if it gets back to your father, he will not be pleased."

"Indeed. Have them thrown into one of the cages with the deigrods," Tristan answered. "Before the blood has dried on their jaws, we will have found the boy and girl."

Chapter 11

Dylan and Emrick arrived at the ridge that overlooked Rosten from afar. From there they could see a small but swiftly moving sphere of luminai moving in their direction.

"I believe we're too late, Dylan," Emrick said.

"I was afraid of that. We're no match if there are Shadow Men. Our only chance now is to hurry back to the mountain and warn Naomi and the young ones," Dylan replied.

"They'll see our luminai, and you know we can't outrun Shadow Men," Emrick warned. "I say we stand and fight!"

"Emrick, this is a fight you know we cannot win. We would only slow them down . . . and not very much at that."

"Then, Dylan, you go. I will hold them off as best as I can."

"Emrick—no!"

"Go! This is the only way, old friend. You've got to save Naomi and our new young friends. They are too important!"

"I won't leave you—"

"Dylan, you have to let me do this for you, and if not for you, then for my family."

In that moment, Emrick's expression shifted into pure determination and Dylan knew then that there would be no use in trying to change Emrick's mind. Dylan had no choice but to respect the choice that Emrick made. He had to let Emrick go.

"You have been a noble friend, Emrick," Dylan finally said after a long pause. "What you have done here won't be forgotten, brother, I promise. As long as I live and longer, the world will remember what you sacrificed on this hill. Take this." Dylan handed him the weapon from his belt still stained with blood from the fallen deigrod.

"That's your best weapon. You'll need it," Emrick insisted.

"You before me, brother. The Shadow Men outmatch you in strength and speed, so you must do all you can to slow Tristan down."

"I will do what I can. I'm not afraid to die, Dylan. I know it's how we face death that matters, knowing that our life meant something for others. Besides, you know a part of me died when I lost Neera and Darus. I'm tired of living in the darkness of this world, and if I play any small part in bringing back the light, then my death . . . even the loss of my family . . . will be worth it."

"You're a man of honor, Emrick. I love you dearly," Dylan said with tears welling in his eyes as they embraced, and he turned away to hasten toward the mountain. Emrick watched the glow of Dylan's luminai staff grow dimmer over the hill until he was left alone in the darkness and waited to make his last stand.

With his weapon ready and clutching his doused luminai staff tightly in his other hand, Emrick knelt behind a cluster of boulders. He knew that he would not walk away from this fight, but he would not give up without unleashing his anger on the ones he held responsible. All of a sudden, Emrick's mind replayed a vivid memory that he had long since forgotten.

The town of Varkos was in disarray. Mothers and children wailed in the torchlit streets as young men were forcefully taken from their homes, led into the center of the village market, and chained together in a mass.

It had only been a few months since the age of darkness had begun. A people that never knew violence had learned to forge weapons for battle, village against village, fighting over quickly depleting resources—that is, until Erikai announced himself as King and brought them under his control with the force of the Shadow Men. The strongest men were enslaved from each village to mine for luminai, and the people were powerless against them.

"Darus, my son, be brave and good for your mother!" Emrick called out from among the line of slaves, feeling like his heart was being ripped out of his body as the little boy sobbed in the arms of his wife, Neera. "I will see you again. I promise. Please don't lose heart."

Neera approached Emrick with tears spilling from her beautiful emerald eyes for one last kiss, but a Shadow Man quickly stepped in between them, snarling angrily at Neera and causing Darus to bury his head fearfully in her shoulder.

"No!" Emrick blurted out, and the Shadow Man turned and looked at him with a taunting glare.

"Move on!" another Shadow Man yelled toward the crowd of men.

More sounds of wailing filled the air as the men were herded out of the village and dragged along from the front. A few men that resisted being chained up and who tried to escape had been struck down swiftly and mercilessly and left to be mourned over by their widows and children under a cold rain.

The coarse iron of the chains chafed his neck, wrists, and ankles as Emrick followed the mass of rain-drenched men out of the village. At the very last moment, he turned back for one last glance of home.

It was so dark that Emrick could not even make out any of the faces that surrounded him as bodies bumped and shoved into each other as they shuffled along together in a heap. A few voices could be heard mumbling among the crowd of men, but mostly it was silence with the Shadow Men growling from time to time, "Keep moving!" and "Faster!" They hiked for miles through the muddy hills toward the Hall of Light Creators, which Erikai had made his royal palace and that sat atop a wide, elevated plateau overlooking the coast to its west.

At last they arrived at the top and stood in front of the large doors of the palace lit up on either side with torches. The doors swung open, and the crowd of men were led into the central chamber glowing bright with luminai torches that lined the massive walls. Through the sea of heads in front of him, Emrick caught a glimpse of Erikai standing above at the top of a grand stairway at the far end of the hall. He cradled an infant child wrapped in a blanket that draped down to the floor.

The crowd halted in front of Erikai, and Emrick peered around at the downcast faces of the other men of Varkos. Across the way he caught the eye of his friend, Dylan, who nodded back.

"Men of Varkos, today your freedom comes to an end. As your king, I will bring order to this new world. And now, behold your Prince!" Erikai said, lifting tiny Tristan into the air above his head.

"Bow before your new masters if you ever hope to see your families again!" roared one of the Shadow Men. The clanking, rattling sound of chains echoed throughout the hall as the men scrambled to lower themselves before Erikai and Tristan.

"Put them with the others," Erikai ordered the Shadow Men.

The men were then herded down a long narrow corridor to a large, ornate iron door that led to tunnels underground where past generations of light creators had long lay buried in a veritable maze of catacombs. The tunnels were low and narrow, and the darkness was illuminated by a few burning torches along the pathway. Emrick passed by a line of chained men from other villages sitting against the walls. They looked up at Emrick through stern and hollow stares. Once all were inside, the Shadow Men shut them in and returned to Erikai who was now sitting on a throne and holding Tristan.

"That is the last of them, my lord," the Shadow Man reported. "All the able young men of the villages have been apprehended for you."

"Good," Erikai replied, but his eyes were fixed on the small child cooing in his arms. "Tomorrow, the mining will begin. Leave several men here with me to serve me, and I want all these statues destroyed immediately," he said, motioning toward the tall statues of the first light creators that stood prominently against the walls of the central chamber. "Put men in charge of each mine, and in time we shall win their loyalty. Then, when Tristan is old enough, I will put him in charge over all of it."

"As you wish, my lord," responded the Shadow Men, but eyeing the young prince with envy.

Waiting in the stillness, Emrick held his breath in the frosty air as he heard them coming closer. He clutched the weapon Dylan gave him and imagined himself hurling it at Tristan the moment his back came into view. Even if he was unable to kill Tristan, he hoped he could wound him enough to slow them down and allow Dylan time to lead Naomi, Zeph, and Laney out of the mountain to safety.

The light came nearer and then passed by. Emrick could make out Tristan and the scout from Rosten, but he was surprised not to see a Shadow Man with them. Emrick lifted the weapon, and the long blade shot out as he swung his arm back over his shoulder with his eyes fixed on Tristan's silhouetted figure moving farther away. Just as he prepared to let go, he felt a tight grip squeeze his wrist almost to the point of snapping it. He was forced to drop the weapon as another hand dug firmly into the sides of his neck and lifted him effortlessly off the ground.

"Prince!" yelled the Shadow Man, as it carried Emrick, choking, toward Tristan and the scout and threw him down hard on the snowy ground at their feet. The Shadow Man handed Tristan Emrick's weapon.

"Let me break him for you, Prince," the Shadow Man growled fiercely.

"Not yet. I want to know who he is first," said Tristan calmly, but with a dangerous light in his eyes.

Emrick struggled to get up on his hands and knees, rubbing his injured neck and breathing heavily as he looked up into Tristan's unfeeling face.

"Prince, we can't waste time," repeated the Shadow Man. "Let me crush this fool, and we'll keep moving."

"No, but make sure he's alone," responded Tristan, and the Shadow Man disappeared at once into the darkness with a low growl. Tristan crouched down eye-to-eye with Emrick.

"Who are you?" he asked, eyeing the weapon as he turned it over and over in his hand and then placed its long, sharp blade under Emrick's chin.

"Emrick."

"Where are you from, Emrick?"

"Varkos."

"And all by yourself, Emrick? Tell me. What would possess you to ambush your Prince like this?"

"You're not my Prince. You never were," Emrick answered with defiance.

"Treasonous words," Tristan said coldly as he stood back up to his feet. "Your King, my father, has ordered that all traitors be killed without mercy on the spot. Are *you* ready to die?"

Emrick remained silent.

"Yes, I do believe you are. You mustn't have anyone or anything you fear to lose?"

"Once," Emrick responded through gritted teeth. "Your father took them from me!"

"I do admire your courage, and yet you attempted to kill me from the shadows? A coward's act."

"He's alone, Prince. There is no one else with him," the Shadow Man said as he returned.

"Interesting. What was your plan? Killing me doesn't solve anything."

Emrick didn't answer.

"Yes, you're protecting someone, aren't you? It must be someone important. Perhaps the two young ones we're looking for?" Tristan turned and motioned to the scout who moved in so he could get a closer look at Emrick's face. "Is this him?" he asked.

"Yes! But there was another one!"

"Indeed. But before we go, I'm going to give Emrick a proper chance to do what he intended to. And you can even have your weapon back," Tristan scoffed as he threw the weapon down on the ground in front of Emrick who grabbed it slowly and staggered to his feet.

"Now's your chance, Emrick of Varkos," Tristan provoked him. "You must have waited for this moment for a long time . . .

imagined what it would be like . . . to take your anger out on your worst enemies?"

"You talk too much!" Emrick responded with a slight, contemptuous bow before lunging at Tristan with all the strength and speed he could muster, swinging his blade and scraping Tristan across the surface of his face as he backed away. With hardly a moment between, Tristan thrust out his leg and planted the heel of his boot in Emrick's chest. As Emrick tumbled back, Tristan wiped his bloodied cheek and winced at the searing pain. "You fool!" he yelled as he charged toward Emrick.

Emrick waited until Tristan was just close enough before making his next move, but this time Tristan caught his wrist with one hand, twisted it, and threw Emrick over his back. Emrick's weapon tumbled loosely from his hand, and Tristan picked it up from the ground as he sauntered towards him. As Tristan prepared to strike again, Emrick pulled another shorter blade out from his boot and plunged it swiftly and deeply into Tristan's side.

Tristan yelled out in pain while sticking his palm out toward the Shadow Man who strangely let out a loud shriek at the very same moment and was moving in to defend him. Emrick pushed the blade in farther, but Tristan swiftly backhanded him. Then, he drove his own weapon into Emrick's gut and pushed him down to his knees, letting him fall limply to the ground.

Tristan slowly pulled out Emrick's blade from his side. Seizing his luminai staff back from the hands of the scout, he touched its hot tip to the gaping, bleeding cut, wincing as it cauterized.

"A valiant fight, old man. I'm sorry your friends weren't here to witness it. Let's go. We'll find his companion and the two young ones at the Bleak Mountains," Tristan said, as they turned and left Emrick alone with images of his wife and son flashing before his eyes.

Chapter 12

After Dylan and Emrick had left them, Zeph and Laney ate with Naomi and rested. Despite everything happening to them, they both slept soundly. When they awoke a few hours later, Naomi was gone. They walked outside together and spotted her about a stone's throw from the shore. She was pulling a long rope up into her boat, at the end of which was a claw-like device. Although she was old, her body moved with youthful vigor. As Zeph thought of missing his own mother, he was overcome with a special fondness for this mysterious old woman before him, this woman he knew nothing of a few days before but whose life was entangled with the whole history and destiny of the world—and now with their past and future as well. He was in awe that she had been able to live out here on her own this long. Zeph stepped over to help her as she rowed ashore, and she looked up at him and thanked him warmly with her eyes.

Naomi reached for the metal claw and pulled it in closer to set it on the ground. She knelt before the claw and dug into it with both hands, sifting through the wet, dark sand until she pulled out several small, irregular-shaped pieces of luminai and placed them in the palm of Zeph's hand.

"How much is out there?" Zeph asked.

"She doesn't know," Laney answered, who had been standing behind them with Wiggin on her shoulder. She paused. "She says she first discovered luminai closer to the shoreline in the shallower parts before Dylan helped her build this device to reach down further in the middle of the lake. Dylan trades it secretly, mostly in Varkos. She says she uses it sparingly for herself, just enough for her to live on, knowing that Erikai controls the supply throughout all the villages."

"Maybe you could also tell us more about the history of this world?"

"She says she wants to know more about us first, Zeph," Laney answered for Naomi.

"There's really not much to tell," he said looking into her kind eyes. "Laney and I have been best friends for as long as I can remember."

"She wants to know about our families."

"Well, I live alone with my mother," Zeph answered and looked down at his feet. "My father went missing shortly after I was born. I never actually knew him. He was taken when Erikai began enslaving men for the mines. Dylan said they met while they were prisoners together. But nobody knows what happened to him after that."

"Daeron," Laney added, after Naomi asked the name of Zeph's father.

Naomi's eyes suddenly grew wider, and Zeph heard a cry of shock come from Laney. "What is it?" Zeph asked. "What's wrong?"

"She knew him, Zeph. She knew your father!"

The color drained from Zeph's face. "You knew him? How? Please tell me!"

"She says we need to know the whole story, Zeph."

"They've summoned you," Naomi said.

"I know, and I'm ready," Erikai responded as he pulled her in closer to himself.

"They can't know about our marriage or our child. You mustn't tell them."

"I won't, my love," he said, kissing her and calmly laying his hand over her belly. "I'm sure Daeron will be there, too."

"Yes I know," she answered, lowering her head and looking away.

"He's with them," Erikai said with a tinge of jealousy. "He doesn't approve of us, you know. It's still you he loves, even though he has his own family now."

"Yes, I know. But I never loved him. Not like that. You know it is you that I love."

"Yes, and I promise that we can still be happy. You don't need them, and they don't need you, but the baby and I need you. Goodbye, my dear. Soon this will all be over," he said as he kissed her again and left, starting his journey to the Hall of Light Creators by the sea.

The haunting sounds of their songs emanating from atop high towers breathed life throughout the valley. Overhead the sky was a deep blue, and the countryside was alive, teeming with bright, colorful flowers and various shapes of trees—a euphoric mosaic of scarlets, indigos, and violets. A flock of broad-winged creatures flew peacefully above, while a large herd of deigrods could be seen running atop the crest of a hill to the south. Long green grass swayed to and fro in the cool wind, and the soothing sounds of a shiny, flowing brook echoed underneath as Erikai crossed an elegant, elevated bridge.

The stone paths and dirt roads were bustling with travelers and business traders leaving and arriving from the other villages. The hillsides were dotted with large, resplendent stone houses and glassy waterfalls, while people tilled happily in golden fields below. Erikai passed by all of this as he approached the bottom of the hill and the path leading up toward the white, imposing Hall at the top.

The large doors to the Hall swung wide open before him as he approached. Erikai made his way across the center of the Hall, which was covered above with a high crystal-clear dome through which the blue sky above reflected down onto a pristine, lustrous marble floor below. As he approached the far end of the room where several light creators sat in tall white stone chairs, Erikai peered at the immense statues that towered above him on both sides that represented the very first light creators.

"Erikai," said Terra, an elegant looking woman with dark red hair. She was dressed all in white and seated among the others. "Thank you for coming."

Erikai gave a stiff, obligatory bow. He glanced over to the side of the room and spotted Daeron standing off by himself. Erikai gave him a sly smirk.

"You must know why we have summoned you here," said Terra, her voice echoing through the hall.

"Yes, to persuade me to end my relationship with Naomi and urge her to return to you."

"It is in her best interest—"

"Yours," Erikai interrupted.

"And of everyone, Erikai," Terra corrected in irritation.

"You've never approved of us."

The light creators all looked at each other quietly, and then Terra responded, "We've never approved of *you*."

"Because of my father."

"Tacitus openly opposed us. He tried to turn the villages against us."

"And you think because I'm his son that I will follow in his footsteps. You don't trust me. This is why you seek to prevent Naomi and me from being together," Erikai said with disgust.

"And instead of respecting our will, you turned her against us and convinced her to leave us!" said Terra as she stood up to her feet.

"You are blind! She left because she loves me and you stood in our way. And *your* will? My father was right! You are corrupt."

"Silence!" Terra yelled out.

"You think you can act as lords over us because you hold the power of light creation," Erikai countered, pointing a sharp finger at them. "It was my father's belief that you have been hoarding this power, when in reality you could teach all of us to harness the energy of luminai!"

"Impossible!" Terra scoffed. "Light creation is passed on by blood. The power is inherited. It cannot be learned."

"Even if it could, would you share it?"

"This world once sat in darkness," she said, noticeably avoiding Erikai's question. "The first light creators brought life to this world, and since then this world has been at peace. There is harmony and abundance for all. There is no want. Why must you cause a problem?"

"And what if something were to ever happen to you?" Erikai asked. "What would become of the world then? Or what need do you have of anyone else sharing this world with you at all?"

"You talk foolishly!" Terra reprimanded him. "Are you threatening us? You are just like your father. He was jealous of our power, and he wanted to rule the world alone."

"Because my father saw that you were corrupt! Enough of this. You cannot get in the way of me and Naomi, and she will never return to you!"

"You will regret defying us, Erikai!" Terra warned.

"Is that so? Is that what happened to my father? Did you get rid of him because he opposed you too?"

"Light creators do not take life, Erikai. We give it."

"Maybe you don't, but others would do your dirty work for you," Erikai retorted back, looking over at Daeron with disdain. "You fools, do you even know why he's here? It's not because he cares about you. He is also in love with Naomi. Isn't that true, Daeron?"

"Erikai, you should listen to them!" Daeron spoke up and moved out into the center of the hall closer to Erikai. "You only care about yourself."

"Nonsense! You're jealous that Naomi has always loved me and never you. That's all! Naomi left of her own choosing."

"Because you deceived her! Somehow you got her to trust you!" Daeron replied.

"It is obvious that we see things differently. I am finished here," Erikai answered as he turned to leave the hall.

Daeron reached out and grabbed Erikai by the arm. "Don't do this," he whispered firmly. "Naomi does not belong with you. You'll never make her happy. She'll see you for what you really are."

Erikai spun around to face Daeron, his eyes a dangerous pool of fury. "Don't get in my way again, Daeron, or it will be the last time. That goes for all of you," he said, sweeping a pointed finger around the room. Erikai tore his arm loose and stormed out to their voices calling after him and the large doors of the hall closing shut behind him.

Upon returning home, Erikai paced angrily around the room, running frustrated hands through his hair. "They will not listen! They won't stop until they see us torn apart and you return. This is not going to end peacefully, I just know it!" Erikai pounded his fist on a nearby table.

"Erikai, what do you mean?" Naomi cautiously placed a gentle hand on his shoulder in an effort to calm him. "The light creators are devoted to keeping the peace!"

"You still believe my father's death was an accident?" Erikai responded, jerking away from Naomi. "My father was right, Naomi. They are selfishly protective of their power. They are not what they should be or as righteous as everyone thinks they are."

"So what do you plan to do?" Naomi said, becoming concerned over his increasing agitation.

"What my father should have done before they took him from me. And I won't let them take you or our baby away from me as well! But first—Daeron."

"Erikai, no! You mustn't!" Naomi cried.

"We can't stay here now. We must bring only what we can carry and what is needed for the child. The light creators have made up their mind and will not stop. They will send someone for you, and we will be gone when they come."

"So Erikai killed my father?" Zeph said, his voice noticeably shaking, after Naomi finished relating the whole story through Laney.

Laney put a comforting hand on his shoulder. "Your father may still be alive, Zeph. She says it was he who created the Shadow Men for Erikai."

"But why would he help Erikai? I don't understand. I thought they hated each other."

"She says your father was the most gifted alchemist in the land. About a year after Tristan was born in secret, which must have been about the time you were born, Zeph, Erikai came back for him and coerced him to create the Shadow Men. Somehow Daeron figured out how to create them from Tristan's blood using ancient magic. It was the Shadow Men who killed the light creators, and then he used them to enslave the men of the villages to work the mines. Only Tristan can destroy them because they are part of him."

"But why would Erikai turn against you?" Zeph asked Naomi. "I don't understand."

"She says Erikai's love for her is the only reason she remained alive," Laney said. "She tried to stop Erikai from going after Daeron. He was filled with such rage toward all of them that his heart became poisoned against her, too. He became paranoid she would betray him and might try to flee with Tristan."

"Was Erikai right?" Zeph questioned Naomi. "Were the light creators jealous of their power? Can it really be taught to everyone?"

"Naomi says the land was at peace but there was some jealousy and rivalry among the light creators. It was rumored that their power could possibly be taught to everyone. The light creators were never meant to be rulers, but the fact that they kept the power to themselves made them rulers in all but name. The Hall of Light Creators was constructed later in homage to their power as gods. She says it is possible that Erikai's father was right about some things."

"But Erikai is mad. He's gone too far! And now Tristan. Naomi, you haven't seen your son since he was born, have you?" Zeph asked.

Naomi answered no with a slow shaking of her head.

"Do you think there is any hope for him? If he knew the truth, could he be changed?"

Laney could feel Naomi's emotion welling up in her own heart. It brought her to the verge of tears. "She wants to believe he can, but he has lived in darkness for so long. He has been a part of so much death and suffering. He is loyal to Erikai just as Erikai was to his own father."

Naomi stood still for a moment and then abruptly took Laney by the hand. "She wants us to follow her," she said, sounding surprised.

"Where?" Zeph wondered.

As if not hearing his question, Naomi grabbed a luminai lantern that hung outside on the corner of her cottage roof. They followed Naomi to a rather steep path that led up the side of the mountain and out onto a broad precipice overlooking the lake covered in darkness. They could only see Naomi's tiny cottage in the distance below, lit up from the inside.

Naomi walked slowly toward the ledge with her lantern in her hand and her back to Laney and Zeph.

"What are we doing up here?"

Then turning back toward the two of them with her hand outstretched, the wind blowing her hair messily across her face, Laney spoke for her with eyes gleaming excitedly in the light of the lantern. "She says it's time, Zeph. She wants to teach me."

Chapter 13

Zeph looked on as Laney took Naomi's hand and led her to the ledge. She told Laney more about how the light was not really created inside her but was a connection to the energy of the luminai that lay deep underneath the surface of the world. She told Laney to close her eyes and feel the ground beneath her feet. Naomi's hand began to feel warmer and Laney could feel a strange energy filling her from head to toe.

Naomi told her to imagine the enclosed valley full of light and color and to sing with the melody that she heard inside of her, which was the song of creation, of light and life. It was Laney's voice that would connect her to the luminai and its energy. As she began to sing, Laney could sense the world beginning to wake up as if after having been asleep for a long time, a world grown old becoming new again.

Laney began to slowly open her eyes. When she did, her vision was startled by all that she could see, which before lay hidden in darkness. She could make out the white sand shorelines surrounding the whole lake, its crystal-clear water, and underneath its gently rolling waves, schools of multi-colored creatures swimming in perfect sync. Lifeless trees around the lake began to slowly straighten and bud bright rosy petals that flew from their branches and were carried by the wind through a light, rainbow mist.

"Laney!" Zeph exclaimed as he walked closer to the edge, squinting his eyes in the flurry of light and vibrant color after having been in darkness for so long. "This is amazing!" Laney did not realize it but Naomi had let go of her hand, fell to her knees beside them, and was weeping. Then, reaching up she took Zeph by the hand and placed it in Laney's. Instantly, he felt as if the world surrounding him was in motion together and that its indescribable beauty was a physical warmth and sensation. There was no joy he had ever known like that which overcame him in that moment.

Laney stopped singing, and the light lingered for a while before slowly beginning to dim and fade until it returned to darkness. She turned to Naomi who was still down on her knees. Zeph helped her to her feet, and Naomi pulled the both of them into a tight embrace.

"She is so happy," Laney said. "Can you believe it, Zeph? I could see everything. Even with my eyes closed, it was like I could still see and feel it all. So warm. So radiant. So beautiful."

"You are the last hope for this world, Laney. I always knew there was something special about you," he said with admiration in his eyes.

They continued to talk about all they had seen and felt before returning down the mountain path toward the cottage. When they arrived at the bottom, Laney placed her hand on one of the woken trees and began to sing. The tree began moving and stretching again as light and color poured up from its roots and onto its new branches. The ground between the white shoreline and the edge of the mountain sprouted long, green and glistening grass. The air was fresh, cool, and smelled delightful, and the surface of the glassy lake breached with creatures as the three, with Wiggin bouncing excitedly on Laney's shoulder, returned to Naomi's cottage.

After the light had faded again, Naomi brewed some tea over the fire using a few of the violet wildflowers that had sprouted at the foot of the mountain, and they sat for hours listening to Naomi share stories from her past through Laney.

As she talked, Zeph noticed something different about Laney. She seemed less like the young girl he knew and more mature in her disposition.

The three of them lost all awareness of time passing. Despite all the hardships that they had faced thus far and all that still stood in the way of peace, their moods were encouraged by these profound moments spent together and by the brief lifting of the darkness to bask in the beauty, color, and warmth of a world returned to light.

Wiggin's ears perked up suddenly, and he flew to perch at the window. He shrieked and began flapping his earwings.

"What is it, Wiggin?," asked Laney, as Zeph instantly bolted up to see what it was.

In the distance he saw a small glow of luminai approaching. "It's Dylan and Emrick! They're back!" he said excitedly as he ran outside the cottage to greet them. After having witnessed light and life return to the world, Zeph and Laney felt as if an entire age had gone by.

As the boat drew closer toward the shore and the light became brighter, Zeph called out, "Dylan!" but strangely no answer came back. He could see the silhouette of a man sitting in the front of the boat with what looked like another much larger figure rowing behind him. Wiggin bounced excitedly, but his screeches and snarls did not sound happy or welcoming.

"Zeph, something isn't right," Laney said, her expression growing increasingly panicked.

The boat struck shore, and the scout in front toppled over dead into the shallow dark waters as a Shadow Man lunged toward a startled Zeph and Laney and grabbed each of them firmly by the throat. Wiggin immediately flew at the Shadow Man with his fangs bared, but he was swiftly backhanded and sent sprawling through the air.

Naomi ran outside toward them with her arms outstretched, but the Shadow Man sent her soaring backward with a stiff thrusting kick and crashing through the side of her cottage in a heap of timber. Zeph struggled to breathe through the bony, cold grip of the Shadow Man clenched tightly around his throat.

"You are the two runaways from Adelaide!" it hissed, pulling Zeph in closer. "Prince Tristan was looking for you. He's on the other side of the mountain and waiting to take you to King Erikai."

Zeph struggled to get free, but the strength of the Shadow Man was equal to ten men. His vision faded to blackness as both he and Laney passed out and were carried by the Shadow Man onto the boat. When they reached the other shore it lifted their limp bodies over its shoulders and made its way back swiftly through the mountain.

Tristan waited with Dylan, whose hands were bound behind his back and a black rope wound tightly around his neck. His face was bruised and his eyes swollen.

"They had better not be dead!" Tristan said angrily, standing up to his feet and walking around behind the Shadow Man. He lifted Zeph and Laney's heads to look at their faces, but his gaze lingered for a moment longer on Laney.

"There was another with them, Prince, an old woman."

"She means nothing," Tristan answered, as he took one more searching look at Laney before dropping her head back down. "It's these two I'm after, that's all. Let's take them back to my father."

After several miles, Zeph began to waken with a terrible headache. He lifted his head up and looked beside him to see Laney still unconscious and lying drooped beside him.

"Laney," he whispered urgently to her over and over.

"Wait!" Zeph heard Tristan say. The Shadow Man abruptly stopped. "I think one of them is awake. Put them down."

It was Tristan who Zeph saw first. He had never been this close to the Prince before. Tristan stood taller than Zeph had pictured, and his upper body and shoulders were much broader. Zeph's eyes followed the black rope in Tristan's hand and were shocked to see the battered face of his dear friend, Dylan, at the end.

"I'm sorry, Zeph," Dylan said with a depressed sound of defeat in his voice. Dylan had always seemed so powerful and confident to Zeph, but now against Tristan and the Shadow Man he was utterly helpless.

"You are the two young ones from Adelaide we've been looking for," Tristan said with a calm, disarming demeanor as he knelt down in front of Zeph.

Zeph lowered his gaze without answering. He was seething with anger inside but felt immovable before Tristan who reached out and grabbed him firmly by the jaw.

"You two fled Adelaide several days ago after the strange light. I want to know what you know, and you will tell me." Zeph looked up into Tristan's eyes but then noticed the recent wound running down the side of his face.

"I've been to the cave, and I've seen the grave. Your friend, Elbor," he continued callously, "he betrayed you! Now tell me, what caused the light?" Tristan followed Zeph's glance as he peered from the corner of his eyes towards Laney who was lying motionless on the ground next to him.

"Tell me!" Tristan demanded. "Your families—you love them don't you? Would you make them suffer for your bravery?"

"You don't understand!" Zeph blurted angrily as he thought of his mother. "There's something you need to know about your father . . . about yourself!"

"I'm not here to talk about myself or my father, but as you won't tell me what I want to know . . . " Tristan stood up and turned his back to Zeph. He nodded toward the Shadow Man whose eyes began to narrow, placing its hand firmly on Zeph's face. Zeph began to feel a strange, burning sensation in his head. He cried out in agony, and everything went black again. He felt cold, dread, and pain. He could almost sense himself being wrapped in darkness like a heavy, coarse blanket, and he had never felt so alone.

But all of a sudden he could see a distant light and hear a faint voice singing a haunting melody that became louder and louder as the light grew brighter and brighter. The pain and coldness began to leave him. A bright figure that looked like Laney was walking towards him. She was surrounded by a sphere of light that grew dimmer until she was standing before him holding out her hand. Zeph reached out to touch it and instantly found himself in front of Tristan and the Shadow Man again. Laney was now standing beside him as her voice filled the air.

Tristan and the Shadow Man stumbled backward, trying to shield their eyes from the light as it enveloped them all and their surroundings awakening with life and vibrant colors.

"Enough!" Tristan yelled. Laney ceased singing, and soon the darkness returned. "It's you!" he said, his eyes wide with wonder. "What was that? How did you do that?"

"There's much that you don't know, Prince Tristan!" Zeph stated.

"Silence! She's the one I want. Take this boy and the old man and go back to Rosten and wait for me there!"

"Back to Rosten? But why?" the Shadow Man challenged.

"I'm taking her to my father. Alone."

"I'm not leaving here without her," Zeph replied defiantly, moving to stand in front of Laney, but before he could react, Tristan plunged his fist into Zeph's gut and pushed him down toward the feet of the Shadow Man. "Take him and go. Now!"

"If you hurt her!" Zeph threatened, looking up at Tristan from the ground and clutching his stomach.

"Zeph, it's okay. He won't hurt me," she said as she looked at Tristan, her eyes softening. "You won't, right?" she asked, expressing compassion toward Tristan rather than fear. She knew that underneath this hardened warrior was a slave to the darkness like the rest of them. Like her, he too, was a light creator. He just did not know it yet.

"Take her swiftly to your father, Prince. We will wait for you in Rosten," said the Shadow Man reluctantly. It gripped a struggling Zeph by the shoulder and shoved him toward the darkness while pulling Dylan by the neck.

"You must tell him, Laney! He must learn the truth! It's the only way!" Zeph called out to her as they faded from view.

Chapter 14

Laney and Tristan were left standing together in the glow of his luminai staff. After a moment of awkward silence, Laney spoke up. "He's right. There is much that you need to know."

"And you will tell me as we have about a day's journey before we reach my father."

"Aren't you going to tie a rope around my neck and drag me along as well?" Laney asked mockingly.

"If I need to." He had not stopped looking at her curiously since the light surrounding them had faded away. He motioned for Laney to walk ahead as he followed behind her. It was silent between them except for the soft sound of crunching snow underneath their feet. They hiked through the hills for miles until Laney finally spoke out, "What will your father do to me?"

"The same thing he does with all traitors I suppose," Tristan responded rather heartlessly.

"But why bring me all the way to him? Why don't you just get rid of me yourself like you've done with all the others?"

"Because you're different—first the light in Adelaide, and now what you did back there. I've never seen anything like it. No one has."

"You are wrong about that, and I'm not a traitor, Prince. Why is your father so fearful of rebellion? Why is he so protective to rule over this cold, dark world?"

"Without my father's rule your villages would be out of control! It is my father who brought an end to the civil wars and all the strife between you."

"Don't you see that it is your father's rule that keeps us all in suffering? It is because of his tyranny that there is no peace."

"Liar—I should strike you for that!" Tristan shouted, but he was surprised when Laney did not flinch but kept walking on ahead of him.

"You don't seem to fear me like everyone else does. Why is that?" Tristan asked curiously.

"Maybe it's because I know you better than you think—even better than you know yourself," Laney responded tenderly.

"Now what does that mean? You've never met me before. I've never seen you. I don't even remember your name!"

"Laney."

"Well, Laney, tell me, how did you do that back there? Where did that light come from?"

"You've never felt warmth or seen color like that, have you?"

"No," Tristan answered calmly as if wanting to say more but couldn't.

"There is much you don't know about this world, about yourself, about your father."

"And how would you know this? You're not older than I am."

"A very special woman told me, the woman we were hiding with on the other side of the mountain when your Shadow Man attacked us and took us away."

"Ah, yes, the strange old woman he spoke of. Who is she?" Tristan asked coldly.

"Or who *was* she?" Laney corrected him as she closed her eyes and sighed to herself, feeling a sudden wave of sadness and pain in her chest well up at the very thought that Naomi might be dead back in the mountain, killed by the Shadow Man. Her thoughts then turned to Wiggin and to Zeph, too, and the reality that she might never see them again added to her pain.

"She was not just a '*strange old woman*,'" she continued as she felt tears filling up in her eyes. "She came from a better past and was the hope for a better world."

"Oh, how is that?" Tristan scoffed.

"I want to tell you, but you won't believe me, and you're not ready to listen." At that moment a strong surge of cold wind blew at them, and in the sky a few miles ahead past the hills they could see dim flashes of lightning and hear slow, peeling rumbles of thunder.

"We need to find shelter soon," Tristan said as if ignoring what Laney had just said. "I know a place nearby."

Coming upon a deep cavern at the foot of a gently sloping hill, they entered inside just as the thunder snowstorm approached. The wind howled and the thunder boomed loudly as they followed the glow of Tristan's luminai staff deeper into the cave.

As they walked, Laney noticed the remains of old wooden carts and metal tools.

"This was a luminai mine once, wasn't it?" Laney asked. "How far does it go?"

"Probably miles. We'll be safe to wait out the storm in here," Tristan said motioning for her to sit against the wall. Tristan sat opposite her, leaning his luminai staff against the cave wall, and pulled back his hood. This was the first time Laney got a full view of what Tristan looked like. She could see Naomi's features in his rugged face, which she found strikingly handsome. Tristan pulled out a few small pieces of dried food and leaned over toward Laney to share them with her, but she shook her head and waved her hand dismissively.

"Suit yourself," he said as he began to eat in front of her.

"How many mines are left in the world?" Laney asked.

"Only a few . . . in the north, near Riskolde. Most have been abandoned now. This was one of the first."

"And what's become of the slaves?"

"Some were freed, some died from the work, and most others . . . " Tristan hesitated, kept his head down, and then took another bite. He could sense her displeasure in what he was about to say. He had never before felt so uncomfortable talking about these things, and for some reason Laney's presence unsettled him.

"And your father keeps all the luminai that's been mined?"

"He dispenses when and as he pleases to ration the supply."

"While keeping most of it for himself," Laney retorted angrily. "And what will happen when all the luminai is mined and runs out?"

Tristan did not answer her. Just then, Laney made out a strange etched marking on the cavern wall just over his left shoulder. Tristan noticed this and turned around to see what she was looking at.

"The sign of the brotherhood. A sign of rebellion," Tristan muttered. The wind continued to howl at the mouth of the cave.

"What is rebellion to you and your father is our hope of freedom," Laney responded defiantly.

This was the most that Tristan had ever spoken with any villager, and he was already becoming intrigued by Laney.

As if knowing what he was thinking she continued, "Yes, if you could spend a moment in our shoes, you would see the injustice. You may think you are on the side of right because your father is the king and you love and honor him, but you must understand how you have been the cause of unspeakable suffering in this world. You've ruined families, caused hunger, death . . . "

Tristan was speechless. In his heart he wanted to lash out at such treasonous talk and defend his father's honor, but he found Laney irresistibly disarming. As she spoke with such passion, he began to notice even more the gentle curves of her face, her stunning eyes in the faint glow of luminai, and the pleasant shape of her mouth as her lips moved.

As if beginning to feel his heart strangely softening toward her through the look in his eyes, she blushed slightly and looked away. "If you only knew . . . " she said as her voice trailed off.

"Knew what, Laney?" Tristan asked. His voice sounded surprisingly sincere.

"What this world was like . . . could be like again. What you saw back there, the light, the warmth, the colors, the life. I know you felt it, too, but you don't know how to describe it. You're afraid of it. Tell me, what do you know about your mother? What has your father told you?"

"She was very sick before I was born and died in childbirth." Tristan's hand clasped the necklace around his neck as he began to speak about her.

"Was that hers?"

"Yes," he answered softly.

"I can't imagine a life without a mother," she said with sympathy, but then her mood quickly changed to indignation, "but what would she think of all the horrible things you and your father have done?"

"She was loyal to father and believed in what he stood for—that his reign, and one day mine, would be necessary for the future of this world."

"Or at least that's what he told you," challenged Laney.

Before Tristan could respond, a low, hideous growl echoed from deeper inside the cavern. Tristan stood up quickly, grabbed his staff, and pointed it in the direction of the strange noise.

"We're not alone."

"What is it?" Laney asked, sounding frightened.

"Not sure, but I remember my father telling me of how the slaves in this mine spoke of something they called the Djavul."

"Djavul?"

"An enormous serpent that dwells in the depths. When many slaves went missing from this mine, others claimed that the Djavul had taken them. My father refused to believe them, thinking the missing slaves had escaped and that the others were lying for them, so he had them flogged."

"And what did you believe?" Laney asked.

The growl bellowed again, but this time the sound was much louder and closer and followed by a low, steady rumbling.

"We need to get out of here, now!" Tristan suddenly exclaimed, as he grabbed Laney by the hand and ran quickly toward the mouth of the cave.

Chapter 15

The Shadow Man led Dylan and Zeph back to Rosten. Now and then it would give a sharp tug on the rope, causing Dylan to stumble down to his knees. Only the Shadow Man could see where they were going in the darkness, and Zeph's efforts to speak with Dylan were forcefully hushed. They walked along in silence except for the low hum of the Shadow Man's breath and Dylan's occasional groans. Zeph's thoughts stayed focused on Laney during their journey to Rosten. He tried to shove out the horrifying scenarios playing out in his head of what could be happening to her.

After many hours, Zeph could begin to make out the dim lights of Rosten in the distance. The village seemed so peaceful from afar, not the menacing place he had always heard about. A scout approached riding atop a deigrod with the other Shadow Man beside him.

"The Prince wishes to keep these two as prisoners in Rosten for now," the one Shadow Man said to the other, ignoring the scout's presence. "Lock them up until he returns for them."

Dylan and Zeph were tied opposite each other inside one of the empty torchlit deigrod cages with their backs against the cage wall and their arms stretched and tied above their heads. Dylan's battered and swollen face hung down wearily. Zeph sat closest to the main road and heard the people of Rosten moving about behind him and whispering to each other. Suddenly, Zeph felt something strike the cage hard behind him. He strained his neck around to see a gathering crowd glaring icily at him and throwing objects at the cage.

An older woman approached and spat furiously at Zeph.

"You've brought trouble on us! It's because of you the Prince and his Shadow Men have come to Rosten! I hope they feed you to the deigrods!" she taunted with agreeable cheers from the others in the crowd.

Out of the corner of his eye, Zeph could see one small boy standing off to the side staring curiously at him. Zeph offered him a soft, reassuring smile, which the boy compassionately returned before disappearing into the darkness.

The angry mob dispersed eventually, and Zeph was left alone with Dylan. He tried to awaken him with whispering calls across the cage, and Dylan struggled to lift his head but did not speak.

Zeph's thoughts turned again to Laney alone with Tristan somewhere in the wilderness on the way to King Erikai. His heart raced at the possibility of never seeing her again, and his mind swirled with anxious questions about Laney that he feared might never be answered. Zeph struggled desperately to imagine a way out of their hopeless situation. He believed that Laney's meeting with Naomi was not by chance, and yet things had turned out worse for all of them. As Zeph thought of this, his head began nodding off from extreme fatigue, his wrists chafing against the thick rope that bound him to the cage. As he fell asleep he began to dream of Laney.

"Laney, I'm telling you, one of these days we're going to get caught!" a younger Zeph said between gasping breaths as he struggled to keep up.

"We're not going to get caught. Trust me, I've done this many times before and they've never suspected a thing."

"That doesn't make me feel any better," Zeph replied.

"Oh, stop being so scared," Laney taunted. Zeph was pretty sure she was grinning as she said it, which made Zeph even more determined to prove to her that he was not a coward. He picked up his pace until they were running side by side.

"So . . . where are we going anyway?"

"You'll see," Laney replied, with an excited smile painted across her face. As they ran, the shadows deepened until Zeph could barely see Laney right beside him.

"Laney, I don't like this . . . "

Laney didn't respond.

"Laney?" Zeph tried again, his tone becoming increasingly panicked. He looked around desperately for any sign of her, but he could barely see anything through the thick shadows.

"Lane—ah!" Zeph screamed as Laney's head suddenly appeared, made visible by her small luminai torch, as she burst into a fit of giggles that turned Zeph's face into a very bright shade of red.

"Gotcha!" she exclaimed proudly.

"You shouldn't have done that! I was frightened that . . . that something bad had happened to you!"

Laney's smile disappeared when she saw that Zeph was serious. His eyebrows were puckered with worry, and his eyes flashed with genuine concern. This confused her. As children, she would always pull similar pranks on him, and after getting over his embarrassment, Zeph would always laugh right along with her. She didn't mean to make him frustrated. Laney looked down at her feet and awkwardly scuffed her soft boot.

"I'm sorry Zeph. I just wanted to have a little fun," she mumbled. Zeph softened at Laney's genuine apology.

"So what were you going to show me?" Zeph asked to perk Laney up again.

Laney's face brightened and she grabbed Zeph by the hand, leading him forward toward a tall stone cylinder structure covered in dark, twisted vines. "This way. Watch your step!" Laney tugged him inside and led him up several flights of a spiraling narrow stairway.

"Where are we?" Zeph whispered, not wanting to know what could be lurking or waiting for them at the top.

"I actually don't know for sure, but . . . " She lowered her voice to a level that Zeph had to strain to hear her next words. "This sure is an amazing discovery, right?"

Zeph wanted to agree with her, but he couldn't shake the feeling that something was very wrong.

"You haven't even seen the best part," she said with anticipation. Zeph managed a rather weak smile and held on tightly to Laney's hand as they reached the top of the stairs. There was an empty stone courtyard that looked big enough to house something. It made Zeph suspicious that nothing was there, or at least nothing that he could see. There looked to be some sort of stone railing encompassing the entire area.

"Over here, Zeph," Laney whispered, which made him realize that she had let go of his hand. He made his way over to the sound of her voice and gasped. Peering through the open air over the edge, they could see Adelaide stretched out below them with twinkles of light scattered like stars throughout the entire village below, which was bustling with activity.

"See? I told you this would be great," Laney said with satisfaction dancing across her expression.

Zeph was speechless. He never knew that his village could look so beautiful. He had always seen it from the ground where everything seemed dirty, but viewed from above it was something to admire. They stood there for what seemed like hours, looking out over their village.

All of a sudden, Zeph felt the hairs stand up on the back of his neck, and he turned to see someone approaching them from the shadows.

"Laney," Zeph whispered, "get behind me. Now." Laney turned and gasped, retreating behind Zeph.

"What are you doing here?" said the low, rasping and ghostly bellow—a dead giveaway for the identity of the black-cloaked figure. *A Shadow Man.* Zeph could feel Laney quivering against his back. "What would King Erikai think if he found you two here?" Its dark figure towered over them.

"Oh! We didn't know that this belonged to the King. We got lost somehow, isn't that right, Laney?" Zeph said, trembling and forcing the words out of his mouth.

"Yes," Laney agreed frightfully.

The Shadow Man let out a breathy laugh, and its eyes narrowed as it lunged at them. "Yes, I do believe you are lost, and I will make sure you are never found!"

Chapter 16

The Shadow Man's chilling voice woke Zeph with a jerk from his sleep. The sounds of clanking metal drew his gaze upward to see the little boy he had seen earlier climbing the cage behind him and fiddling with the thick ties that bound his hands.

"What are you doing, kid? Go on, they'll see you!" Zeph whispered urgently.

The little boy paid no attention and continued working busily to free his hands. Zeph looked around but did not see the Shadow Men or any other people of Rosten around. Only one street torch remained lit.

Zeph felt the tightness around his wrists release—his hands were free! Before he could turn around, the little boy dropped a small sharp tool on the ground beside Zeph, jumped down, and dashed away. Zeph quickly crawled across the dirt floor of the large cage to Dylan and tried to wake him.

"Dylan! I'm free. We're getting out of here!"

Dylan's eyes opened but he looked rather disoriented.

"Zeph," he struggled to say as a crooked smile formed across his mouth while Zeph began to slice through the ties around his wrists and neck. "I'm so sorry," Dylan mumbled with tears beginning to fill his eyes. "I tried to . . . "

"I know Dylan. Don't worry about that now. Someone has taken pity on us and helped us, but we don't have much time. Shadow Men will be close by."

Zeph helped Dylan slowly up to his feet. They could hear the sound of sleeping deigrods in cages nearby. A few men lay passed out against the outer wall of the cages with their hands loosely gripping empty mugs.

Zeph heard a sound and turned to see the shadowy silhouette of a person at the door of the cage as it swung open.

"Come quickly!" came a soft female voice.

Zeph hesitated, but seeing that there was no other option, he followed the girl with long, curly red hair out of the cage, half-carrying Dylan as they walked down a narrow, dimly-lit lane of shanty cottages. She looked all around before opening the door to hurry inside one of the cottages where the little boy waited in the center of a room lit with candles and a fire.

Zeph laid Dylan down on a soft chair in a corner of the room as an older woman brought in steaming bowls of broth from the next room. Zeph ate it up heartily and fed some slowly to Dylan as he lay propped up slightly on a tattered pillow.

"I'm Keani. These are my children, Ava and Wren. They told me that Shadow Men had brought two strangers here and had them locked in deigrod cages."

"I'm Zeph from Adelaide. This is Dylan of Varkos. Why are you helping us? I didn't know there was a kind soul in all of Rosten. You are both very brave," Zeph said as he placed his hand on Wren's little shoulder and warmly thanked him with a smile. Wren just looked intently back up at him with timid eyes. "We are certainly grateful, but you are all putting yourselves in danger," Zeph continued, speaking to Keani.

"Varkos," Keani breathed. "A woman with her son came through here a long time ago from Varkos. I believe her name was . . . Neera. They stayed with us for a short while. Said they were looking for her husband—"

"Emrick!" Dylan gave a strangled cry.

"Why yes! I believe that was his name," Keani answered. "You knew them then!"

"Emrick is our friend," Zeph answered. "What happened to them?"

"I don't know. They just moved on," said Keani.

After a long pause and glancing toward Zeph with deep sorrow in his eyes, Dylan responded, "Emrick died saving my life."

Zeph looked at Dylan with shock, and his heart ached with compassion for his friend's loss. Turning to the others, Zeph began to explain the whole story. Many times, his voice broke up and his eyes welled up with tears as he thought of what had become of all his friends, especially Laney.

After he was finished and wiped the salty tears from his face, Keani spoke up, "I don't believe our meeting is by chance then. This gives me great hope. We need to get you out of Rosten so you can save your friend, Laney."

"But how? Prince Tristan already has a head start, and his Shadow Men will be watching over this town and the gate carefully. Chances are, they already know we're missing."

"Go, Zeph. Save Laney. I'll stay here. I will only slow you down," Dylan interjected.

"But how will I get past the gate?"

"I know another way," Wren's quiet raspy voice suddenly spoke up. Keani's lip trembled as she reached out and pulled the boy in close, burying his head against her chest.

"You have courage," Dylan answered, patting him on the shoulder.

"I will prepare things for your journey, Zeph," Keani said as she began to fill up a bag for him. "We don't have much luminai to give you, but you can take what little we have hidden away."

"I don't know how to thank you," Zeph said.

"Just find your friend," she replied, as she placed the bag over his shoulder. "That gives me hope. Wren can take you to the border of Rosten, and from there follow the wall and just keep going in that direction." She ran her hands through Zeph's tousled hair and embraced him, which reminded Zeph of his mother.

"Be strong, Zeph," Dylan urged, seeing fear in his eyes. "This is all happening for a reason. Since I have met you I have seen things play out that I could never have imagined. Things are not all as they seem. Keani is right. Me finding you, Laney meeting Naomi, and now the surprising kindness of this family—just when we thought things couldn't get any darker, the extraordinary has happened. We may all have more scars to show by the end of this, and I don't know what pain or loss still awaits any of us, but I've also seen such acts of faith and love without which a better future wouldn't even be possible." Zeph nodded with newfound courage and Dylan struggled to his feet to embrace him.

All of a sudden, a loud commotion could be heard outside the cottage toward the center of the village near the cages. Keani peeked her head out of the door and saw the two Shadow Men and several villagers with torchlight approaching cottages at the beginning of the lane.

"Quickly, you must go now!" Keani exclaimed, closing the door. "I will delay them. Ava, douse the fire and show Dylan into the other room. Get him out of sight!" Keani flung her shawl over her shoulder and prepared to run out the door.

"Keani!" Zeph said, grabbing her by the elbow, his face showing disapproval at what she was about to do.

"It's the only way. Come right back, Wren," Keani said, hiding her head under the shawl, breaking free of Zeph's grasp, and darting out the door.

"Help! Help!" Zeph could hear her yell as she ran down the lane toward the approaching Shadow Men.

Zeph slowly inched the door open and watched as she ran up to them. He could not make out what she was saying, but after a few moments, the Shadow Men and the crowd with them turned around and went away.

"C'mon!" Wren said, tugging on Zeph's sleeve with one hand and holding a small lit luminai torch in the other.

Zeph followed him in haste out of the cottage and in the opposite direction of the crowd, frequently peering back over his shoulder. They moved swiftly across the thin layer of snow, passing the rows of cottages until they found their way to the dark borders of the village and a stone wall about three times Zeph's height.

"What do I do now? Is there a loose stone or a hole to climb through?" Zeph asked, peering near the ground at the bottom of the wall.

Wren did not utter a word but only looked toward the very top of the wall.

"Climb, huh?" Zeph responded reluctantly as he grabbed one of the sturdier vines that clung to the wall and began to carefully make his ascent while Wren stood by holding the torch as high as he could to provide some light.

A few times Zeph's foot slipped on the wet vines and stone, but he made it to the top safely and turned around to behold a wide view of Rosten.

In the loudest whisper he could, he called down to Wren, "Thank you for helping us. Now go on, get home to your mother!" Wren gave him one last smile before he turned around and started running in the direction of his home. From high above, Zeph watched Wren's light disappear into the shadows of the cottages and then turned around to look down the other side of the wall into the pitch-black darkness below.

Chapter 17

Tristan ran with Laney away from the menacing sound that shook the cave. They could feel the warm breath of the Djavul blowing behind them. Large chunks of the cave ceiling began to fall, and one of them struck Laney and knocked her to the ground. Tristan turned around swiftly, waving his luminai staff as the Djavul reared up, its large fanged mouth opening, bellowing a deep guttural growl. Tristan glanced aside at Laney who appeared to be lying unconscious near him. He pulled out his blade and hurled it at the Djavul, merely bouncing it off his armored skin. Its huge head lunged swiftly forward at Tristan, sending him tumbling backward. It slithered closer and prepared to attack again when a bright, warm, and colorful light filled the cave with the echoing sounds of an ethereal voice. The Djavul screeched, shuddered, and backed away. Tristan was surprised to look over and see Laney standing, almost as if floating off the ground, her arms outstretched at her sides.

The cowering Djavul slithered back into the shadows and deep down into the cave. In a moment all was quiet and calm again. The melodic voice diminished, and the light faded, leaving Tristan and Laney alone again in the glow of his luminai staff. Laney's eyes closed and her head fell to one side as her whole body began to tumble limply toward the ground. Tristan rushed toward her and fell to his knees by her side.

"Laney!" He called her name several times, but there was no response. In the light of his luminai staff, he could see her face covered in dirt and blood as he brushed away her hair. Knowing the Djuval might return, he retrieved his blade, strapped his staff to his back, and put his strong arms underneath Laney's limp body. He lifted her up and carried her out of the mouth of the cave into the fading remnants of the passing snowstorm. He knew he could not carry her all the way back to his father like this, so he decided to head toward the village of Riskolde by the sea, which was just a short hike through low rolling hills to the north.

Without the protection of the Shadow Men, Tristan felt vulnerable and wanted to avoid recognition of his identity. He hung his head low and hid his face underneath his hood as he approached the gate to Riskolde. The village lay at the bottom of a hill at the edge of the sea and was surrounded by steep cliffs. The village was the smallest of the four. The people were net casters, but trade with other villages had ceased after the wars.

A few men with long spears and torches of fire met Tristan before he reached the gate.

"Who are you?" one of them asked indignantly, pointing his spear directly at Tristan. He was taller but much older. Tristan could detect fear in his voice.

"She's hurt. I need to find a place for her to stay," he answered quietly.

"Well, you are not welcome here. Move on," gruffly answered the other man, chewing on a piece of root weed. He was younger than the other, thin, but appeared just as trepid.

"Please, don't make me ask you again," Tristan responded firmly.

"Let them come with me, Osian," an older woman's voice suddenly spoke a little further from behind Tristan. He was surprised that he had not detected anyone else before.

"But, Catrin, you know . . . " one of the men began.

"Shush," she interrupted. "Riskolde cannot turn away an injured person seeking help. You should both be ashamed of yourselves. Follow me, sir." Catrin gestured towards Tristan with a warm smile and a slight twinkle to her soft brown eyes.

The men stood there quietly as the old woman walked past them without a care, and Tristan glared at them underneath the edge of his hood as he followed her through the gate. They passed through into a courtyard lined with cottages oddly stacked on top of each other along a cold, windy path that led down to the edge of the sea. The town was quiet except for a few people moving around. Some cottages glowed with candlelight.

"My cottage is just here, up these stairs." Tristan followed the old woman up a winding set of steps and through the narrow doorway into her small cottage. She led him over a creaky, wooden floor into a back room that had a small table and a bed. Tristan was relieved to finally set Laney down, removing the luminai staff from his back and propping it against the foot of the bed. After a while, Catrin brought a blanket warmed by the fire to cover her.

"What happened to her?" the old woman asked curiously.

"She fell," Tristan said softly, his head still hung low.

"Well, I will warm up some broth for her to eat. You can just sit and wait with her."

Tristan just nodded, and Catrin left the room. He did not want anyone to know who he was, but this made him feel uncomfortable. He was left alone with Laney now. His heart felt a strange, surprising concern for this young girl he had just met. His mind went back to their conversations and to the mysterious light occurrences. He was intrigued by her and kept watching her face for signs that she was waking up.

After a while, Catrin came back in with a steaming bowl and handed it to Tristan.

"This is for you."

"I'm not hungry," Tristan refused.

"Nonsense. You carried that girl here. This will strengthen you and warm you up."

Tristan accepted it from her hand reluctantly and started to eat.

"So where are you two from? Are you Varkosian?"

Tristan just shook his head. The old woman peered at Laney and then back at Tristan, eyeing him suspiciously.

"Where were you coming from when you came up behind us?" he asked her, trying to deflect the attention away from himself.

"I went to visit my son . . . Brycon. He's buried in a grave out beyond the village with the others."

"What others?" Tristan asked. Catrin's expression morphed into an age-old sadness.

"We lost a lot of our children a few years back to fever." She fell quiet. "Can I get you some more broth?"

"No," he replied, handing the bowl back to her.

"This village. You have no supply of luminai here?" Tristan asked her.

"It's been a long while since our trader has received any supply from King Erikai."

Tristan reached into a small pouch that hung on his belt at his side and handed her several blue luminai rods. Her eyes widened. "For taking us in," he said, responding to the look on her face. Then he leaned in closer toward Laney.

"Thank you, sir," Catrin answered as she turned to leave the room, but she knew he didn't hear her for he seemed to be focused on the young girl that lay on the bed in front of him.

After several minutes Tristan came out of the room. The old woman sat in a chair by candlelight as if waiting for him. She looked up and smiled. "Sir?"

"I'll be back later. Where can I get a drink in this village?"

"Follow the path down to the sea. But be careful. You stick out, sir, and there are many Riskoldians who don't like strangers much."

"I'll be fine," Tristan answered back and left the cottage. Descending the steps, he pulled up the warm black wrap around his neck to cover half of his face and began walking in the direction of the sea. His mind swirled about as his thoughts were preoccupied with the girl he left behind in the cottage. He had never felt this kind of concern for another living person like this.

He heard children crying in cottages, and a few people looked at him suspiciously as he walked by, but he kept his head down. The air was colder as it blew in off the sea. Coming to the end of the stone-paved path that was covered by a light frost, he saw a dim, candle-lit building that wreaked of root weed. He bumped past a few other men stumbling out noisily into the street as he walked inside. The place grew quiet and Tristan could feel piercing eyes looking right through him. He found an open table near a burning fire pit in the middle of the room and sat down, putting the long blade from his belt down on the center of the table.

"What'll you have, stranger?" a sweaty, heavy-set and bearded man asked, approaching Tristan cautiously.

"Something hot," Tristan replied without looking up.

"Well, how about some tea then?" the man asked, irritated with Tristan's demeanor.

Tristan nodded. The man said nothing and walked away. Out of the corner of his eye, Tristan could see him walk over to a table in the corner and begin talking with several sturdy men seated there. Several moments later, he returned with a small steaming pot and a steel cup and put it down in front of Tristan.

After drinking for some time, and knowing he was being watched, he turned to face the men in the corner. "Can I help you, gentlemen?"

Simultaneously they all stood up together, walked over to Tristan's table, and sat down. The one directly across from him leaned back and put his dirty boots up on the table, taking Tristan's weapon out of its sheath and beginning to examine it. Tristan's hands balled into fists under the table, preparing to strike if the men made one sign of aggression.

"Look at that, would ya," the man scoffed as he displayed it to the others seated next to him. He started swinging it around in the air. "This is quite a weapon you've got here, stranger. I haven't seen one like that in Riskolde before."

"Better be careful with that," Tristan said through gritted teeth.

Then leaning in, trying to peer under Tristan's hood to get a better look at his face, the man whispered, "What are you doing here?"

Tristan took another sip of tea, but one of the other men pushed the pot and cup off the table, causing an eruption of laughter around the table and other eyes around the room to peer at them.

Tristan sat quietly for a moment as the men continued to laugh, but then all of a sudden he thrust out his fist toward the man's throat causing him to choke and gasp for breath. Tristan swiftly grabbed his weapon, threw the table over, and kicked one of the other men off his chair, placing the sharp blade stiffly against the throat of the one man left seated.

"Sir!" yelled a woman's startled voice from the door. Tristan turned to see Catrin running in with wide eyes. She grabbed him by the arm that held the blade.

"What is it?" he asked irritated, not taking his eyes off the three startled men.

"The girl, sir! She's waking up!"

Chapter 18

With the small luminai torch Keani had put in his pack, Zeph scaled down the other side of Rosten's outer wall and stayed within arm's reach as he followed the length of it.

Zeph had no idea what he would do when he found Laney. He was no match for Tristan or the Shadow Men, but he also knew he could not hold back from doing something regardless of how the end for him would be written. He held fast to a faith that his efforts would not be in vain, and this hope drove him on.

Soon he reached the edge of the wall and could see all the way down its long, curved stretch toward Rosten's illuminated gate. He knew that he had to be careful of the scouts and to avoid being detected by a deigrod.

Zeph got down on his hands and knees and crept slowly, keeping the light of his torch close to the ground as he snuck away from Rosten. Once he felt he had created enough distance from the gate, he got up and started running and did not look back until he reached the crest of the hill. He could see Rosten faraway below. Relieved that he had made it this far, a surge of confidence filled him with energy and he kept moving with a swift stride.

Since Zeph had met Laney, this was the farthest apart from each other they had ever been. Barely a day went by when they did not see each other in Adelaide. Now that he was alone in the darkness for the first time, the thought of where she could be right now filled him with a burning anguish. What if he was too late? A panic rose up in him. *No*, he thought to himself, *I can't think like that.* Zeph shook the thoughts out of his head and willed himself to keep going.

Just as Dylan had said, so much of their journey this far was surprising and inexplicable. Several days ago, if he had been told all that would happen to them and the people they would meet who were tied to their past, he would never have believed it. Zeph's thoughts turned to the Shadow Men and then to Tristan, and he felt stormy rage brewing up inside him. They had taken away all that he loved. He felt nothing but hatred for them, but how could he stop them?

After about an hour of walking, Zeph began to have the eerie sense that he was not alone in the hills and possibly even being followed. Maybe his escape from Rosten had been too easy. He stopped in his tracks, bent low to the frosty ground and doused the luminai torch while listening intently to the silence and stillness that surrounded him. After a few moments, he began to hear the sound of crunching footsteps approaching slowly, saw the dim outline of a tall figure holding a firelit torch move past him about a stone's throw away, and then it faded away.

Strange for a man to be out here alone like that, Zeph thought to himself. He laid still for quite a while before pushing himself back up to his feet, relighting his torch and continuing on. He had only taken a few steps when he heard a menacing snarl and whipped around to see a deigrod leaping swiftly at him. No match to outrun its speed, the top of its head rammed solidly against Zeph's back and sent him tumbling to the ground.

Zeph rolled over and pushed himself up, wiping the blood, cold snow, and mud from his face.

"What are you doing all the way out here, boy?" the scout atop the deigrod said, holding out his torch as the large beast circled around in front of Zeph and moved in closer with a low growl. A frosty mist blew from his nostrils. "You must be one of the prisoners who escaped, aren't you? Well, what will they think of me when I bring you back?"

"I'm not going back," Zeph retorted. "You'll have to kill me."

The scout laughed heartily and jumped down off the deigrod. Patting the beast on the top of the head as it slowly sank into the ground on its haunches, he walked over toward Zeph, whose head just came up to his chest, and eyed him up and down. Laughing again, he said, "Don't be a fool, boy! I *will* take you back dead or alive, but it doesn't have to come to that."

"I'm not going back there," Zeph repeated.

"You're rather brave for such a small one. Then again, you would have to be brave to come out here all by yourself. Where's your friend? The other one?"

Zeph remained silent and did not answer.

"All right then," the scout said as he grabbed Zeph firmly by the back of the neck and began to drag him toward the deigrod. Zeph yanked his head away and swung around to run the other way.

The scout pulled out a sharp blade from his side and lifted it above his head to strike at Zeph. At that moment the deigrod sat up with a loud roar as something hurled from the darkness toward the scout and tackled him to the ground. The deigrod reared up on its hind legs, and Zeph saw the figure of a man standing up between him and the beast holding the scout with the point of the blade curved at his neck.

"Tell your deigrod to back down!" the voice commanded, which Zeph immediately recognized. "Get his torch, Zeph."

"Emrick?!" Zeph said, surprised. "But we all thought you were dead!" Zeph walked over and picked up the torch still in shock to see his friend alive.

"Almost, lad. Now tell me, what are you doing out here?"

"So much has happened since I last saw you."

"Where is Laney? Dylan?"

"Dylan is in Rosten. He was severely hurt by Tristan and the Shadow Men. We were captured and taken to Rosten, but we were freed . . . by a woman and her children who knew your wife and son!"

Emrick's face shifted from shock to happiness, and his mouth opened several times, but no words came out. Finally, Emrick's face settled on pure joy and tears began to pour out of his eyes. It was the first time Zeph had ever seen Emrick express such warmth as he explained to him the story.

"Why are you out here alone, Zeph?" Emrick's voice had taken on a husky tone, marred by the emotions welling up inside him.

"Tristan has Laney and he's taking her to King Erikai as we speak. I'm on my way to help her, although I don't know what I'm going to do when I get there."

"Then it was fortunate that I found you here, isn't it? I shall go with you, and we will use this deigrod to get there faster. Won't we?" Emrick asked, leaning closer toward the scout's ear, who grunted as Emrick plunged the edge of the blade firmly into his back.

"Where have you been since we last saw you?" Zeph asked.

"I don't know how much Dylan has told you, but when we got back to the other side of the mountain, our friends were dead and the scout was missing. We followed him to Rosten but we were too late. We spotted Tristan and the Shadow Men leaving the village on their way to the Bleak Mountains. I tried to slow them down so that Dylan could get back to warn you all to escape. But Tristan got the better of me and left me, he assumed, for dead. I don't know how long I was out or what gave me the strength to revive. But I eventually woke up and headed back for the mountain hoping to find you."

"Did you make it back? Did you see Naomi?"

"I saw her home damaged, but I couldn't find her anywhere."

"And Wiggin?"

"I didn't see him either, Zeph. So I headed back out hoping to find you and the others."

Emrick nudged the scout up on the crouching deigrod, and he and Zeph climbed on behind him. The beast rose up on all four paws. "If you value your life, you will do exactly as I say and not try anything stupid," Emrick said, whispering into the scout's ear.

"We need to hurry!" Zeph said.

"You heard the boy," Emrick shouted, and the scout muttered a word to the deigrod that made the large beast lunge forward and begin to run at a quickening pace in the direction of Erikai's palace.

Chapter 19

"She woke up asking for you," Catrin said as Tristan followed her into the room to find Laney still lying on the bed, breathing slowly and her eyes half opened. He felt a strange relief to see her awake.

"Did you give her something to eat?" Tristan asked Catrin without turning to look at her.

"Yes, I did, sir. She ate very little. Said I needed to find you . . . had something important to tell you."

As Catrin left the room, Tristan pulled up the chair beside the bed and looked earnestly at Laney.

"I thought you had left me," she whispered, her eyes blinking slowly.

Tristan shook his head and just looked into her eyes. To his surprise, he felt his heart jump at the worried tone of her voice. *Almost as if she wanted me to stay . . .*

"Are you still taking me to your father?"

"I have to," Tristan answered, looking down.

"What has happened to my friends? Are they alive?"

"They are being held in Rosten. The Shadow Men are awaiting my father's orders."

"He will kill them, won't he?" Laney asked, her eyes holding a tiny flicker of hope that her assumption was wrong.

Tristan said nothing but nodded and the disappointed sigh that escaped Laney's lips was almost enough to break his resolve.

"There's something you must know, Tristan."

"You just need to rest so we can leave."

"Why don't you just carry me the rest of the way?"

Tristan blushed and stuttered, "I can't, it's too far . . . " Then he stood up and proceeded to walk out of the room.

"Tristan, please," Laney said, calling out after him. "Just listen to what I have to say and then you can take me to your father."

Tristan hesitated and then returned to the chair.

"Your mother . . . she's alive."

Tristan's eyes furrowed, and then he scoffed, "That's not funny." He stood up and shoved the chair back to leave. Laney reached out and grabbed his hand.

"It's the truth. The woman within the Bleak Mountains where you found us. She's been hiding there for a long time. I've waited for the right time to tell you." Tristan looked in Laney's eyes and knew she was telling the truth, but the shock held him in disbelief.

"That old woman? That's impossible," he uttered, shaking his head, but his voice was beginning to crack. "My mother died giving birth to me." Laney could sense the hurt underneath Tristan's hardened exterior.

"That's what your father told you, but he's been lying to you, Tristan. Your mother is special. What you saw me do, she could do, too. She taught me how."

"What? I don't believe you. I don't believe any of this!"

"Your father kept her a secret from you all these years."

"Why? Why would he do that?" he angrily insisted. "My father loves me!"

"I don't doubt that he does," Laney answered. "But your father is the reason why this world is in darkness. Years ago he murdered people like your mother, like me, who had the power to create the light you saw. He buried them all in the tomb we found near Adelaide. That's where the light came from that sent you on a search for us. But that's not all. You have this power, too, Tristan, from your mother."

"What are you saying?"

"I am saying you have a power inside you that can change the world to make it better for all again."

"What do you mean *again*?" he asked.

"Your father has been hoarding knowledge and power for himself and it has been the cause of great suffering and injustice. He is deceived in believing he is right in doing so, but his pride has suppressed the one truth that can breathe life back into this world again. What you saw—the light, those bright colors, that warmth—it can be true everywhere and always again only if . . . "

"Stop! I don't believe any of this!" he shouted.

"You don't or can't?" Laney whispered gently in response.

"Is everything all right in here?" Catrin asked, peeking in through the door. Tristan just turned and glared at her from under his hood, plainly irritated.

"When I return, we leave to go to my father!" he said, storming out of the room and pushing past Catrin.

Tristan's mind raced furiously as he walked down the lane away from Catrin's cottage back toward the sea under a dark sky of lightly falling cold rain. He shook his head, trying to muffle Laney's voice inside his mind and the words that kept replaying that she had spoken to him. *Impossible! Impossible! Lies!* He kept telling himself, but he could feel it getting harder and harder to deny.

As he walked past the drink shop, the men he scuffled with were just leaving together, spotted Tristan walking past, and began to follow him in the shadows. He had no idea where he was going, but he could not stay with Laney and listen to her telling such tall tales. Yet he also could not deny that Laney possessed a special, unexplainable magic over him—not only in her power to create light but also in her ability to soften his hard heart. He fought against it. His mind went back to when he first heard her sing and was bathed in the warmth of the light. Deep down he desired to know more, but he was afraid. Since he had met Laney, a whole other part of him that he had not known was there had come out, a sympathy, a compassion, a love that went beyond duty or loyalty. And his mother? Could she really still be alive? Of course he wanted this to be true, but that would mean that his life up to this point was all a lie and that his father was not the man that he loved. Why would Laney lie to him?

Tristan turned down an alley that ran between two rows of stacked cottages and passed by an old man laying against the wall. His clothing was tattered and he was covered in a dirty blanket, muttering something unintelligible with his eyes glazed over. Tristan thought of what Laney said, "better for all." All of a sudden he saw this poor man differently than he would have before. He would have stepped by coldly without even noticing, but now he felt something he had not felt before—pity. Where was this man's family? Did he have a place to call home? How had he ended up like this?

Tristan noticed in the man's hand a root weed pipe, which he gently took from his fingers. The old man did not move or flinch. Tristan eyed the pipe with a new curiosity. It was the old man's escape from a life of suffering.

Suddenly Tristan felt a hard, sharp pain on the back of his head. Turning over on his back, he saw in the dim light three men standing above him. His head was ringing from the blow, his eyesight was blurry, and the sound of their antagonizing voices and laughter was muffled. He tried to get up but was struck back down followed by several stinging kicks to his ribs. The last thing Tristan felt was a bottle being shattered over his head before the world faded away to darkness.

The three men dragged Tristan's body out from the alley and down to the sea and laid him out in the shallow cold water, left to drift on his back near the shore in the darkness. The men walked away laughing and congratulating themselves, still clueless as to the identity of the stranger they had attacked and left for dead.

The icy water woke Tristan, but he could not move much. He could only sputter out the cold, salty water that flowed across his lips. Some men standing by had watched it all happen. They waited to pull Tristan out of the water and further up on the shore once his attackers had left. Tristan could barely make out the sound of their voices. His wet face was uncovered, as one of the men stooped down holding a candle-lit lantern above him.

"I've seen 'im before! It's Prince Tristan!" one exclaimed.

"No, couldn't be 'im," replied the other.

"I swear it."

"Why would he be here? He's never without 'is Shadow Men!'" one said, looking around, with a sound of fear in his voice.

"I don't know, but it's 'im. We better do something to help 'im or if King Erikai finds out, they'll be no one left alive in Riskolde," one of them insisted.

They carried Tristan back to one of the men's cottages and laid him out on the floor by a warm fire.

"What 'ave you got here?" his wife asked. "We can't take 'n a stranger!"

"It's the Prince, dear! Some fools roughed 'im up, left 'im for dead in the sea. If we didn't do something, we'd all have to pay!"

"We should remove 'is wet clothes before he catches fever," the wife stated.

"And disgrace the Prince? We'll do no such thing!" the man replied.

"Oh, he sure is a 'andsome one!" the wife stated as she began drying his head with a towel.

They all watched him curiously. Tristan lay still for a long time, his chest moving up and down slowly with each breath. In his dreams, Tristan saw glimpses of Laney, his father, and then an old woman wearing a mask over her mouth whom he did not recognize. He asked her who she was, but she wouldn't speak. She pulled off the mask, revealing that she did not have a mouth at all. Tristan looked sadly into her eyes, the same color as his own, and as he did he heard the name "Naomi, Naomi, Naomi" grow louder and louder in his head. He sat up next to the fire abruptly, startling the man and his wife out of their chairs. He stood up, and still dazed, fell into a shelf knocking its contents to the floor.

"Where am I?" he demanded, lunging clumsily toward the man and pressing him against the wall.

"I'm sorry, Prince Tristan," the man said, lowering his face not to make eye contact. "We found you in the sea and—"

"How long have I been out?" he demanded, beginning to wheeze and cough.

"For 'ours, my lord. We brought you here to—"

Before the man could finish, Tristan stumbled out of the cottage. His head continued to throb as he wandered back up the road and made his way up the stairs into Catrin's cottage, storming past her into the room where Laney still lay on the bed. Her eyes grew wide when he entered. His clothes were still partially soaked.

"Can you walk?" Tristan demanded.

"What happened—"

"Can you walk?" he repeated to her stiffly.

"Yes, I think so."

"Then, we leave for my father now!"

Even in the dim light, Laney could see Tristan's eyes looked sick. "You don't look well," Laney answered with concern.

"I'm fine!" he insisted as he placed his luminai staff on his back and began to pull Laney up off the bed and toward the bedroom door.

When they entered the next room, Catrin saw for the first time Tristan's full face in the candlelight, recognized him, and immediately prostrated herself on the floor. "Prince Tristan! I didn't know . . ."

Tristan looked at her, paused, donned his hood, and then mumbled, "Sorry for the trouble." He turned to leave.

"Thank you, Catrin," Laney said, walking over and kneeling down in front of her. She lifted her head and kissed her. "Bless you!"

Catrin was still in shock and looked back and forth from Laney to Tristan, who stood waiting by the door. "You be safe, miss," she finally said, never taking her eyes off of Tristan.

Laney smiled, gave her another kiss on the forehead, and got up to leave with Tristan.

Tristan did not speak as they walked together toward the gate of Riskolde. Laney noticed that he did not walk with the same stride, but appeared to struggle wearily to stand upright and coughed with almost every breath.

The two men standing by the gate eyed them curiously as they approached.

"Well look who's awake," one of them said, eyeing Laney.

Tristan led her on but heard the men mumbling and chuckling about something to themselves. As he and Laney left Riskolde behind them in the distance, the men called out after them, taunting at them from the gate.

"You'll never make it like this," Laney said after some time had passed.

"We've already wasted too much time. I won't make my father wait any longer."

"But you aren't well."

"We are not going back, and I'll be fine," he replied defiantly.

"Your father is going to kill me if you take me to him. You know that, don't you?"

Tristan was silent. He stole a glance at Laney and her face was angled towards the ground. She looked disappointed, as if she was expecting more of a reaction from him. At that moment, Tristan's resolve to take her to his father momentarily weakened but he quickly hardened his heart. "Well," she continued, "I want you to see the look on his face after I confront him with all I've told you. Maybe then you'll believe me, even if it's too late."

Tristan did not answer. *Lies*, he repeated to himself. The fondness he might have felt for Laney turned to anger. *Why was it affecting him so much? He knew none of it was true. Why would he listen to some peasant girl from Adelaide over his father?* Yet, the more he tried to ignore it, the more his mind spun with confusion and doubt. Deep down he was anxious to ask his father about it all and curious to see how he reacted. He believed that would settle it forever and quiet the agitation in his spirit. No more lies.

Chapter 20

Tristan led Laney further inland away from the coast, leaving far behind the frosty wind and fading firelight of Riskolde by the sea as they journeyed northwest through hills of lifeless, mangled trees towards his father's palace. Laney could sense that Tristan was struggling at his present pace, and with every few breaths, he let out a raspy, wet cough.

"We should stop—," Laney started, but Tristan cut her off abruptly.

"Keep moving. We only have a few hours more to go."

"You won't make it. We both know it," Laney answered, turning and looking at him directly in the eyes under the glow of his luminai staff. Tristan did not say a word. He noticed a genuine concern in her eyes that made his heart skip and held him still for a moment.

"Keep . . . moving," he insisted, darting his eyes away from her soft but powerful gaze.

Silently they followed a winding, dry riverbed for miles and wandered through a steep ascending slope dotted with large boulders. Tristan's strength grew weaker with each step, and he knew that at any moment he might not be able to stop Laney if she tried to escape.

As they cleared the ridge, they could see across several tiered hills in the far distance the bright aura that illuminated Erikai's palace, which Laney had never seen before. It was truly the most magnificent structure her eyes had ever beheld, having known only the simple wooden shanties in the villages and several old stone houses that lay in ruins that surrounded Adelaide on the outlying hills.

Tristan felt the strength suddenly leave his legs. His head spun, and his vision began to fade. He reached out and grabbed Laney by the arm as he slumped forward onto the ground, dropping the luminai staff.

"Tristan!" Laney yelled out as she tried to brace his fall and then carefully turned him over on his back.

Her voice sounded muffled as she continued to call his name, and the image of her face became blurry as his consciousness slipped away. The fear of death suddenly seized him. His hand reached out to touch Laney's face, which caught her by surprise, but she instinctively grabbed it and held it against her soft cheek. Tristan struggled to stay awake, shivering, and he mumbled something that she could not make out before his head dropped back and he passed out.

Laney frantically laid her ear against his chest. She could hear his heart weakly beating as a light snow began to descend on the crest of the hill. She removed her cloak and covered him with it, propping the luminai staff up against a nearby stone. This intimidating warrior who struck fear in so many was now helpless and resting in a deep and peaceful sleep. He was not a threat to anyone now. His face to her looked handsome and serene.

This was Laney's moment. She could enact revenge on Tristan for all the hurt that had befallen her world, her family, and the loss of her friends. His life was in her hands now, and she could take it if she pleased.

But thoughts of revenge were fleeting, and in that moment, Laney did not see a ruthless killer or a heartless tyrant, but a life to be loved. She looked intently into Tristan's face as her heart swelled with compassion. Her mind replayed all that Naomi had told her, and her heart broke again for all that Tristan had lost without even knowing it—the truth about his mother, his father, and himself. Laney lifted his head into her lap as she began to hum a tranquil melody, and light encompassed them in a warm glow. Tristan's body began to twitch, and she could see his eyelids shifting as he began to dream.

Tristan was looking up into the face of a strange but lovely woman in whose arms he was cradled as she sang a pleasant song in a bright and colorful room. He did not know who the woman was but he felt calm in her arms. Then into view appeared a face that reminded him of his father, though much younger. He spoke to the woman with firmness in his voice, but his words were muffled as if he was talking under water. Tristan was laid down, and the faces and voices became distant. He could hear them growing more tense.

Images flashed before his sight—images of his younger father, stooping down to look closely into his face, saying something he could not make out, and then taking him by the hand and walking him through the palace.

Then, he was standing behind the Shadow Men. Their backs were turned to him, but he could hear their whispers and taunting laughter. He reached out and pulled one of them by the edge of its cloak, but when it turned around Tristan found himself staring up into his own disfigured face.

Tristan woke up to Laney singing over him. He sat up abruptly and pushed away from her with a surprising surge of strength.

"What are you doing?" he exclaimed in protest, startled by the light.

"You lost consciousness," Laney said, looking into his eyes with a slight blush, and the light surrounding them slowly faded back to darkness.

Tristan struggled to answer, his mind still trying to separate the vivid dream from reality as his weakness returned. "I need to talk to my father. Now." He tried pushing himself up slowly to his feet with a coughing fit, reaching for the luminai staff nearby. But not yet able to stand, he slumped down with his back against the hard rock.

"You dreamed and you saw her, didn't you?" Laney asked, as she sat next to him a few feet away. Tristan eyed her curiously but a wave of emotion rushed through him.

"Who?" Tristan looked off into the distance ahead.

"Your mother."

Tristan paused, and then quietly mumbled under his breath, "I didn't see anything." Laney knew he was lying.

The wind howled through the hills, and the two sat together for a while in silence. Laney continued to look out of the corner of her eye at Tristan, wishing she could get inside his head in that moment. She could sense that he was wrestling with his thoughts, and he could feel the weight of her fixed attention. There was so much more she wanted to tell him about his mother. She opened her mouth and started to speak, but Tristan interrupted her. "Your mother . . ." he faltered, trying to deflect further questions about it. "What is she like?"

Laney's mouth curved into a soft smile, thinking of her mother. Even though Tristan was avoiding her question, she was touched by his willingness to act interested. "Well, she's wonderful. She's the kindest person I've ever known, and she always knows how to cheer me up and make me laugh."

"What was it really like . . . growing up in Adelaide?" Tristan responded as if not listening to what she had just said, but the question bothered Laney.

"You've seen it," she answered with some indignance. "What do your own eyes tell you? Our people are poor and hungry. We often go days without luminai, and the darkness and the cold . . . tell me, Prince," she shifted, "how can you and your father live the way you do knowing how the rest of us suffer?"

The question upset Tristan but he did not know how to answer her and could not offer any defense. Tristan's perception had changed since he met Laney. He used to not care about anyone else but his own father and doing what pleased him. Having spent this time with Laney, however, he began to see things differently. A world of once nameless masses of poor villagers was now before him this lovely, unique, and mysterious girl who did not cease to have a strange, powerful, and growing effect on him.

"And your friend Zeph . . . what does he mean . . . ?" Tristan blurted out.

Laney was taken aback by the odd question, and she shifted nervously. "Zeph's been my best friend since we were children." Tristan could hear sadness creep into her tone as she continued talking about him. "We've always made the best with what little we had. I honestly don't know what I would ever have done—or would do—without him," she said, suggesting with her tone that if Zeph's life was in danger, he was at fault. This made Tristan uneasy, but he was not sure if it was the sting of her accusation or the affection she expressed for Zeph that troubled him most.

Yet for all that Tristan had done, even toward those most precious to her, there was something that kept Laney from despising him. She could not shake off a genuine compassion she felt toward him. She deeply and sincerely wanted him to be saved, to know and to believe who he truly was, even allowing him to take her to his father if it was the only way. Maybe the tenderness she felt was the fact that they shared something special in common. They were the last light creators.

While she pondered all of this, she noticed that Tristan had since become quiet, except for the sounds of his strained breathing. His head slowly drooped down until it slumped and rested against her shoulder. She could not help but laugh to herself at the irony of this moment as she sat awake in the darkness, waiting and thinking of what lay ahead in her future and for the fate of the world.

Chapter 21

"It's been days, and we have not seen or heard a thing from my son or the other Shadow Men," Erikai pondered, his voice echoing through the vast hall. "Surely he will return soon with good news, and whatever this disturbance was, it will all be over. Still, I can't seem to rid myself of the premonition that something is not right about this situation." Erikai's brow furrowed as he contemplated his concern.

The two Shadow Men that stood with Erikai in the courtroom each began to cough and wheeze. One of them keeled over.

"What's the matter with you?" he asked them curiously.

"My Lord, I feel weak," replied one.

"Me as well," agreed the second with a shiver. "I feel cold."

Erikai turned to one of the guards nearby, "Fetch Daeron!"

A few minutes later, the guards returned dragging a thin man, his wrists and ankles in shackles, barefoot and wearing tattered clothes. His long hair covered most of his face and a dirty beard hung down to the middle of his chest.

"Daeron, something is wrong with the Shadow Men. They appear to be sick. What's going on?"

Daeron slowly inched his way toward the Shadow Men, pushing the hair away from his face and looking intently at them. He then turned to Erikai and said gruffly, "Tristan is sick, my lord. Looks like fever."

"What? My son! What can be done?"

"Nothing I'm afraid. The life of the Shadow Men is bound to Tristan. What happens to him happens to them."

Erikai descended the stairs toward Daeron and grabbed him firmly by the shoulder. "Do something or my son could die!"

"I can't do anything without Tristan here, my lord."

"Daeron, the great alchemist," Erikai scoffed. "You are a fool!" he yelled, striking him across the face and knocking him to the ground. "Get him out of my sight!" The guards picked up Daeron and led him back to the room where he had been kept a prisoner since darkness fell upon the world.

Erikai slumped on his throne, "Tristan, my son!"

Time passed and there was no change to the Shadow Men or Erikai's mood when the doors to the courtroom suddenly burst open and the guards proudly announced the arrival of Tristan who entered the hall with Laney. Erikai sat up immediately and ran across the hall to greet his son who sunk exhausted into his father's embrace.

"Tristan, my son! Bring food and drink and get Daeron right away!" Erikai said, turning to the Shadow Men and guards. He had not even noticed Laney's presence as he remained focused on Tristan, whose face was pale and beading with sweat. "My son, you have returned. I was growing worried about you." It was then that Erikai turned to face Laney. "And who is this?"

"She's the one you sent me to find," Tristan replied, finding it more difficult to get that statement out than he thought it would be.

"Oh," he said and paused, his eyes squinting with a sinister gleam. "So you are the cause of all the trouble, are you?"

Laney did not respond.

"Come, let's hear all about it," Erikai said, walking Tristan across the hall and seating him on the steps. Laney's eyes searched her surroundings as she followed behind them. She had never been in a place lit up by so many luminai torches before, and she was in awe of the height of the walls after living for so long in a small, cramped cottage. What remained of the statues caught her attention. Her thoughts turned to Naomi, Zeph, Dylan, and Emrick, remembering all that she had learned about the history of the world. Now that she was here, she wanted to know even more. She tried to imagine what the room would have been like in the age of light. It was almost as if she could hear the echoing song of the light creators in the distant past still ringing and filling this hall of stone.

Erikai motioned to the guards. "Take her away. I want to talk to my son alone," he said, grasping Tristan warmly on the shoulder. "I will decide what to do with her soon."

One of the guards grabbed Laney by the arm and began to pull her away.

"Wait!" Tristan shouted, holding up his hand.

Erikai looked at Tristan with surprise. "Son?" His voice had a sudden sharp edge to it.

Tristan sighed heavily and coughed. "Tell him, Laney!" Tristan demanded.

Laney looked back at Tristan, stunned.

"Tell me what, son?" Erikai halfway scoffed and then looked at Laney. "Well, out with it then!"

"I think he needs to hear it from you," Laney retorted back.

Tristan breathed another heavy breath. "She says she met my mother . . . " He sighed. "In the Bleak Mountains. Is this true?"

"That's preposterous! Your mother died long ago, giving birth to you, Tristan. You know that."

Tristan continued, undeterred. "She says mother had the power to create light in this world, and that there were others also. She claims you ordered the Shadow Men to murder and bury them out of sight. That was the tomb I found, wasn't it?' Tristan asked suspiciously. "What did you do to my mother?"

"Tristan!" Erikai stood abruptly and turned his back. Then he looked at Laney and pointed, "You would believe the lies of this ignorant girl whom you just met over your own father?"

"I want to know the truth!" Tristan shouted.

"I've told you the truth! And after all I've done for you, son!" Disappointment and anger flickered across Erikai's expression.

At that moment, the guards and Shadow Men walked into the courtroom with Daeron.

"Ah yes, Daeron! Please help my son. He is delirious!"

Laney turned and looked at the thin, weak man standing in chains between the Shadow Men.

"Daeron?" she asked, peering at him with astonishment. "You're . . . you're Zeph's father?"

Daeron looked at Laney with wonder. "Zeph? You know my son?" he asked, a hint of joy replacing the look in his aged blue eyes—eyes that looked just like his son's.

"Yes!" Laney smiled. "Zeph is my best friend!"

"Where is he?" Tears began to stream down his face.

"He's being held prisoner in Rosten!"

"Enough!" Erikai interrupted, grasping Laney by the arm and shoving her toward the Shadow Men. "Take this girl and her lies away! Daeron, I called you here to take care of my sick son!"

"Laney!" Tristan yelled out, trying to stand up on weak legs but falling down. Their eyes met, and a look of desperation passed between them. The Shadow Men appeared to be struggling to stand up as well. Tristan looked at them curiously. "What's wrong with them?" he asked his father indignantly, but Erikai did not respond.

Tristan did not understand how, but he now realized that all this time his life had been somehow connected to theirs.

"Laney!" Tristan yelled to her. "Show my father!"

Laney's eyes widened as she understood what Tristan was telling her to do. At once she began to sing as they led her away, and instantly a light poured out from her body and encircled them. The luminai torches lining the walls of the courtroom began to glow brighter with so much effervescent light and color that it shocked everyone's eyesight, including the Shadow Men whose grip on Laney loosened to the point of almost letting her go.

"A light creator? Impossible!" Erikai yelled, enraged. "Shadow Men, destroy her!" he commanded them without a moment's hesitation.

One of the Shadow Men thrust its hand out toward Laney and clutched her throat, causing her song to end and the brightness to fade.

"No!" Tristan yelled with all the strength he could muster. He drew his blade, but was too weak to reach the Shadow Man or fight as he stumbled toward them. His eyesight began to blur, and he could barely make out his father's form. But he could hear his voice echoing, "Tristan, my son, don't be foolish! Finish her off quickly," he commanded the Shadow Men.

Tristan knew what he had to do. He plunged the blade into his right arm, letting out a guttural sound as both Shadow Men yelled out in pain. The one restraining Laney by the throat suddenly dropped its arm, grasping it in agony.

"Tristan!" Erikai screamed, his voice cracking. "What are you doing?"

Tristan could see the dim figure of his father moving quickly toward him reaching to take the blade away. Tristan looked at Laney one last time and whispered her name before closing his eyes and plunging the blade deep into his chest. He could hear the Shadow Men shrieking in pain as they crumpled to the floor. He could hear Laney screaming his name before his world faded to black.

"No!" Erikai cried, picking up a lifeless Tristan in his arms. "My son!" He suddenly turned to Laney with ferocious anger in his eyes. "You! What have you done?"

Erikai stood up and rushed toward Laney, growling with seething hatred, but at that very moment, the doors burst open to the echoing roar of a rearing deigrod who charged swiftly across the hall toward them. Zeph gave a command to the scout, who ordered the deigrod to attack the guards, which he did easily with a brush of his large paws. Emrick jumped down with the scout, still holding the blade at his back, to face a defenseless Erikai.

"You fools! This is treason!" Erikai screamed at them.

Emrick turned and saw the fallen Shadow Men and narrowed his eyes at the lifeless body of Tristan. "It's finished, Erikai. Your kingdom ends today."

"You don't understand!" Erikai argued. "I did what was right for this world! The light creators are not what you think!"

"Your self-righteousness and greed have brought nothing but darkness and pain," Emrick replied adamantly. "You separated me from the ones I loved, and I never saw them again. It is only mercy that spares me from killing you myself right now. Look around you. This brokenness is because of *you!*"

Zeph ran towards Laney and embraced her, overcome with joy. Over his shoulder, she could see Tristan's body lying on the ground. Zeph was surprised to feel her hold suddenly loosen and let go of him, as she ran to Tristan's side.

"Laney? What happened here?" Zeph asked her.

She gently lifted Tristan's head to rest in her lap as she brushed Tristan's hair back from his face, tears beginning to stream down her cheeks. "It was Tristan, Zeph. He did it. I told him the truth. He didn't believe it at first, but he defied his own father and saved me. He saved all of us. He took his own life to defeat the Shadow Men. They're gone. Forever. We're free." Her voice broke on those words, and something in her heart shifted when she looked at Tristan.

A tear traced its path down her cheek, lingering there for a moment before it fell. She gently laid her forehead on his and closed her eyes. "I love you," she whispered, quiet enough that no one else could hear. She began to hum, her voice marred by the ache in her heart. As she hummed, a soft glow emanated from Laney that spread over Tristan. The light began to retract until it was centered around his chest and then flowed into his heart. Laney kissed Tristan's forehead, her final goodbye to him, and opened her eyes.

She stood up to face Zeph. His eyes held hers, and there was a flash of jealousy and shock there that surprised her. But he buried it and quickly looked to the fallen Shadow Men. Once so strong and fearful, they were nothing now but lifeless heaps on the floor. Zeph also noticed the man in shackles shuffling towards him, sobbing.

"Zeph, meet your father," Laney said eagerly.

Zeph's eyes widened as he realized who the man really was, a man he had only heard stories of as a child. "Forgive me, son," Daeron pleaded. Zeph broke into a run and wrapped his father in a firm hug, his eyes welling up with tears.

The sounds of Erikai's cries of lament echoed throughout the hall in the warm glow of luminai. The pain of separation and the anger of loss was mixed with the joy of reunion and the hope of freedom. A paradox of emotion filled the room in which one age now ended and a new one began.

Epilogue

Zeph wandered through the crowded market of Adelaide with his luminai torch, looking for Laney. For a brief moment he turned his gaze down the dim alley road that led to Elbor's shop. Anger welled up in his spirit, but he was not yet ready to face Elbor and call him out for his lies.

Zeph's memories flooded back to the many times he had chased Laney through the marketplace, and all at once he knew exactly where he might find her. He made his way toward the gate and ascended the hill as a light snow began to float down. He came upon Laney sitting alone on the ledge among the ruins of the old stone house that had been their shared overlook for so long.

I'm just an ordinary girl. Why me? Laney thought to herself. Memories of Tristan flooded back to her mind, bringing back the familiar ache to her heart and a painful expression to her face.

"What are you thinking about, Laney?" Zeph asked, concerned at the look on her face as he approached her.

"Nothing," Laney answered, acting surprised and shifting uneasily. Zeph could tell she wasn't telling the truth, but decided not to push more for an answer.

"So, what will we do now?" he asked, sitting beside her.

"Look for Naomi and Wiggin. If Emrick didn't find them, they must still be alive somewhere. She needs to know what Tristan did, that it was her son who saved us all."

"Emrick should be returning with Dylan soon. When are we going to share the news with everyone? Erikai's reign is over now and you have a gift to share with the world."

"Soon. We will bring the good news to the villages and persuade them to join with us. We need everyone's help, but it will take time and patience. We need to teach them and rebuild their trust in each other and . . ." Laney paused.

"And what, Laney?"

"Zeph, I just believe there is much more to the story behind this world and the mystery of our place in it, and I really want to know. Will you help me?"

"Of course!" Zeph answered, grabbing Laney's hand and squeezing it endearingly.

"You've been my best friend, Zeph," Laney responded, letting go of his hand. She jumped down off the ledge and started to walk back down the hill toward the village.

Zeph noticed that she began to hum a familiar tune, but he couldn't place where he had heard it before. He looked curiously at her as she walked away. She had been different around him since they reunited, and it bothered him.

"Are you coming?" she said, turning around to face him. Her eyes glistened in the light of his luminai torch.

"Where's your torch?" Zeph asked. "How'd you find your way up here in the dark?"

"I don't need one anymore."

Of course, Zeph thought to himself. *Won't the world be amazed when Laney begins to show them what she can do?* Zeph felt a sense of pride that he knew her best.

Zeph walked her back to her cottage and they parted with a tender hug.

"I'll see you tomorrow, Laney," Zeph called out to her. She turned towards him with the familiar challenging grin on her face.

"If you can catch me first."